The God Mockers

And Other Messages From the Brownsville Revival

Stephen Hill

Revival Press

An Imprint of
Destiny Image® Publishers, Inc.
P.O. Box 310
Shippensburg, PA 17257-0310

ISBN 1-56043-691-3

For Worldwide Distribution
Printed in the U.S.A.

This book and all other Destiny Image, Revival Press, and Treasure House books are available at Christian bookstores and distributors worldwide.

For a U.S. bookstore nearest you, call **1-800-722-6774**. For more information on foreign distributors, call **717-532-3040**.
Or reach us on the Internet: **http://www.reapernet.com**

Dedication

Recently, I heard a man with deep emotion in his voice explain that when he first received the Lord there was no one close by to personally disciple him. He had no one to lean on. He had no one to speak into his life. Consequently, not long after his initial experience with Christ, he fell away from God. Now, over 20 years later, he was coming back to Jesus with tears in his eyes at the revival meeting in Pensacola. I thought to myself, *What a tragedy to begin the Christian life without being surrounded by godly men and women. What could this man's story have been if he had been instructed in the ways of God by faithful soldiers of the cross?*

I thank God that early in my Christian walk, the Lord encompassed me about with solid, faithful, on-fire men of God. This book is dedicated to two of those men: Reverend James R. Summers, Executive Director of Outreach Ministries of Alabama, and Reverend Herb Meppelink, the former Executive Director of Mid-America Teen Challenge in Missouri, currently Executive Director of South Texas Teen Challenge.

Gentlemen, thank you for enduring hardship as good soldiers. Thank you for not flinching in the heat of battle.

As generals in God's military, thank you for imparting your years of Christian experience into a young, green private. Thank you for keeping the faith. Thank you for believing in young men and women whom society had given up on. To you, I dedicate this manuscript.

Contents

Foreword

This book forms a sequel to Steve Hill's first collection of sermons from the Brownsville Revival entitled *White Cane Religion*. And if the *White Cane Religion* messages are hot (and they are!), the messages in this present volume are hotter.

This reflects the progress of the revival itself: From month to month, its flames are burning brighter, its effects becoming deeper and more widespread, and the consequences of rejecting or scorning it more severe. In other words, God is upping the ante! *The revival is intensifying.* Steve Hill's burden is intensifying too. His passion for the Lord and for the lost is all-consuming—and this after two years of preaching at least four nights a week, in addition to running an international ministry.

I have worked side by side with Steve now for the past 12 months, and the saying that familiarity breeds contempt simply does not apply here. (In fact, it does not apply to *any* of the sacrificial laborers who give themselves unstintingly to the work of the revival at Brownsville. The more you get to know them, the more you are impressed with the dedication of their lives before the Lord.) Night in and night out, as all of us on the ministry team labor together for souls, pushing ourselves to the limits of physical strength, Steve faithfully leads the way, always putting the lost and backslidden first, urging them to come to the altars to repent and find mercy, painstakingly demolishing their excuses and confronting their pride—*every single night*. (This has been repeated more than 400 times now in the past two years.) And the enduring fruit has been absolutely glorious. The uncompromising word brings uncompromising results!

As you read the living messages in this vibrant book, you will not need to wonder what this evangelist means. He will speak to you with perfect clarity and with no holds barred. And if the words wound you, don't draw back in denial or fear. Instead read on and respond. Whom the Lord wounds He will heal—and His healing will outlast time.

So, take this book in your hands and begin to dive in. But before you do, pray the simple prayer that Steve leads his hearers in every night: "Dear Jesus, speak to my heart; change my life. In Your precious name, amen." Be assured that He will answer your prayer. Prepare to hear and be changed!

Dr. Michael L. Brown
May, 1997

Chapter 1

The God Mockers

"What did you think of the service?" the pastor asked. One of the three church members who had come with him to the Brownsville Revival warily answered, "Well, what did *you* think of the service?"

The minister opened the passenger door of the car and confidently said, "It was all right, but all that shaking— *that ain't nothing. That ain't God.* I can shake too. I could shake on my own. You just watch." Then he settled into the front seat, and the others quickly took their seats in the car to see what the minister was about to do.

The men watched wide-eyed as their pastor began to mock the move of the Spirit they had all seen in the revival service that night. The man began to shake and tremble, scornfully imitating some of the more than 1,000 people who had responded to the altar call. The driver turned out of the Brownsville parking lot and had gone only a few yards down the road when in the middle of his mocking demonstration the church pastor suddenly screamed, *"Stop the car! Please, stop the car!"*

The other men in the car watched, shocked and fearful as their pastor fumbled with the door latch and literally fell out of the car onto the hard pavement of the city street. They were dumbfounded when he began to desperately wail at the top of his lungs: "Forgive me, God! Forgive me, God. Forgive me, Lord!" The men now knew their pastor's mocking imitation was over. No one could imitate the sorrow in that man's voice.

After God's judgment visited that pastor, one of the men from the car that night returned to the revival and received a genuine touch from the Lord. It was this man who came to me in tears and shared this sobering story. Friend, if you have been guilty of mocking any revival or work of God in any man, woman, or child, you don't know what you're doing. You don't know *who* you're dealing with.

When you presume to judge someone who has been filled with the Holy Ghost, *beware*. When you dismiss the testimony of someone who has been set free from drug addiction or pornography, *beware*. When you ridicule those whose bodies are twitching or shaking under the influence of God's glory, *beware*! Have you forgotten that God's Word and the annals of Church history are filled with the supernatural dealings of our supernatural God?

Unusual manifestations accompanying life-changing encounters with God are intertwined with the revivals that birthed virtually every mainline Christian denomination in America and the world! Anytime you analyze something and quickly come to the conclusion that it "can't be God," be careful. You are not mocking that person—you're dealing with Almighty God. Heed the stern warning of the apostle Paul:

> *Do not be deceived, God is not mocked; for whatever a man sows, this he will also reap. For the one who sows to his own flesh shall from the flesh reap corruption, but*

the one who sows to the Spirit shall from the Spirit reap eternal life (Galatians 6:7-8 NAS).

I am constantly asked, "Why are you so intense?" Frankly, I am tired of the rapes, the killings, the child molestation, and the drug addiction. I'm tired of seeing broken families and disintegrated marriages. I want Jesus to come down. I want Heaven to come down. I want America to be saved. I am intense and the situation is urgent because this is a matter of life and death. (Pastor, if you don't have that same urgency in your heart and voice, then you need to change professions.)

The Lord recently spoke to my heart with these words: "Preach what I have placed upon your heart. Do not hesitate. Do not put it off. Remember, Steve, you will not face man on Judgment Day. You will face Me. You will be held accountable for every word and deed...I am doing a deep cleansing work. Speak, My son, to the darkness. There must be Light for Me to continue My work. Many are cloaked in the darkness of sin...Just as I spoke to the darkness and the Light overcame it, so speak to sin and My Spirit will overcome it. I will forgive today. I will heal their backslidings. I will deliver those in bondage. I will create life where there is death. This is a new day."

It was shortly after this that God gave me this message on "The God Mockers." You are probably thinking, *Well, it's obvious that this chapter is not for me. I'm not a God mocker; I'm a God lover. Sure, I might be a little rebellious in a few areas, but I certainly don't oppose God.* You also might be feeling the hand of God on your conscience right now because you know you mock God daily. I have good news for you: God is going to do a work in your life.

Although thousands of people come to the Brownsville Revival from other countries across the globe, most of the visitors—1.5 million at this writing—live in the United States. This is a country where rapists are set free on the smallest of technicalities, where convicted serial murderers can avoid justice by pleading insanity. Once they serve seven or eight years in a mental hospital, they are set free to kill again! (And many of them do.)

Americans who commit armed robbery may receive a ten-year term in prison, but most will be pushed out on the streets early due to crowded prisons. They then return to their professions armed with even more tricks they learned in prison. Friend, the United States is too lenient. Be careful not to be too lenient on yourself. It will damn your soul.

What do you do when the Word of God is preached? Do you open up your heart and say, "Lord, I bare my innermost being to You. Speak to me"? Or do you say, "Well that certainly doesn't apply to me. Who does that guy think he is?" If you alienate yourself from God's Word and refuse to receive correction and rebuke, you may be a *God mocker*.

If you are stumbling over the word *mocker*, you should know that this word appears in various forms at least 50 times in the Scriptures! It usually refers to people who scoff at, jeer, jest, or make sport of other people or things. Now, remember Paul's warning in Galatians 6:7. God says He will not be mocked. Whatever you sow, you will reap. Centuries earlier, Isaiah the prophet said, "...be ye not mockers" (Is. 28:22a). Another prophet, Jeremiah, said, "I sat not in the assembly of the mockers..." (Jer. 15:17). The Scriptures picture mockers as *those who oppose God*. Period.

A mocker has a rebellious attitude. He may even mock God to His face (the most dangerous method), in an act of blatant rebellion (and stupidity). Pilate's soldiers cursed Jesus and hurled foul abuse at Him the day He was crucified. They threw a robe on Him and mocked Him saying, "If You're the Son of God, tell us who slapped You?" (see Lk. 22:63-65) That's mocking. You are probably thinking to yourself, *Well, I've never done that*. Careful, friend. You're letting yourself off too easy.

Mockery isn't limited to open ridicule and scoffing. The student who sits in a class with his arms folded looking straight at the teacher may be a *silent* mocker. He may nod his head, but inwardly he is rebelling against everything he is being taught. Paul said, "Be not deceived" (Gal. 6:7a). This implies we *can* be deceived because the human heart possesses an inherent tendency toward self-deception. We can even deceive ourselves concerning our relationship and condition with God. That means you may think everything is okay when it really isn't!

God discerns the very thoughts and the intents of the heart. He knows who you are and what you've done. You just can't put anything over on God, and you will reap what you have sown. If you've sown seeds of rebellion, you will one day harvest a field of thistles and thorns. If you've sown seeds of discord among the brethren, you will reap some terrible consequences. Friend, if you've jeered at God, scoffed at His servants, or stuck up your nose at His Spirit, you are about to reap some grim results. *Mockery has never been a fruit of the Spirit of God, and it never will be!*

My final definition of a *mocker* will bring this uncomfortably close to home. A mocker is also someone who sees something or someone and considers it *worthless*. Foolish men treated the Son of God like He was worthless. They arrogantly hurled abuses at the One who took away the sin of the world! The God mockers shouted, "If Thou be the Son of God, come down from the cross" (Mt. 27:40b). Friend, you can do the same thing with your life.

Matthew Henry wrote years ago, "If we sow to the wind, we shall reap the whirlwind. Those who live a carnal, sensual life rather than one that honors God, should expect no other fruit than corruption, ruin and misery." Billy Graham referred to "sowing to the wind" in his prayer at President Clinton's first inauguration: "We have sown to the wind. We're reaping the whirlwind." Unfortunately, history is riddled with the sad stories of prominent God mockers who suddenly found themselves at death's door. The French writer and infidel, Voltaire, lived in the 1700's during the violent French Revolution. He spent much of his life opposing God and ridiculing Christians. On his deathbed, he said, "Doctor, I will give you half of what I am worth if you will give me six months to live." The doctor replied, "Sir, you cannot live six weeks." Voltaire blasted back, "Then I shall go to hell, and you will go with me!" A short time later he slumped over and died.

Pastor Bausch of Cloverdale, New York, knew a God mocker who constantly cursed Christians. He would say, "Show me a hair on the palm of my hand, and I will show you a Christian." The same man sang a different tune when it came time to die. His last words were, "I am in the flames! Pull me out. Pull me out!" Another dying God mocker said with his last breath, "I have treated Christ like a dog all my life. He will not help me now."

The Marks of a God Mocker

The first telltale characteristic of God mockers is that they mock God with their *lifestyle*. They may not want to admit what they are, but their actions give them away. "I'm not a mocker, Brother Steve. I don't walk around spitting out curse words." No, but is your life a curse word? Does your lifestyle mock the face of God, throw a whip upon His back, and crucify Him afresh every day? *God mockers scoff at God's way of saving sinners.* We hear them every day: "Surely God won't do that. He just doesn't do things this way. It's embarrassing."

God mockers mock holiness by saying, "Who do you think you are? Are you a 'holier than thou' hypocrite?" They don't realize that they aren't just mocking a person—they are mocking the living *Christ* in that person! That is a dangerous place to live, and an even more dangerous place to die. What do you think when people say they've been set free from bondage? Do you say, "I wonder how long that will last?" These comments mock the power of the Blood and the cross! You might as well look up at Jesus and taunt Him with the words, "It will never last." God mockers scoff and hold in contempt everything they "don't approve of."

The second mark of a God mocker is a fear of confrontation and change. They are so stuck in religious tradition that they are closed to new revelation. The pastor who mocked God as he left the Brownsville Revival was steeped in religious legalism. He was in bondage and totally closed to the moving of the Holy Ghost. (How anyone can come into a revival meeting in Brownsville and fail to feel Jesus is beyond me! I can't imagine it.)

If this revival doesn't exhibit all of the classic ingredients of revival, please talk to me, friend. What more do you have to offer? Every night, hundreds are seen falling on their faces before God in repentance of their sins. Each week souls are being saved by the hundreds. Often by surprise, people are being filled with the Holy Ghost. Ministers of various denominations from around the world are coming here, being touched by God, going back, and seeing the Spirit ignite fires of revival at their home churches. If that is not beginning to touch 'all flesh,' what is?

If you are critical of the Brownsville Revival today, what would you have said about the outpouring on Azusa Street under William Seymour? If you had lived 100 years earlier, would you have tried to shout down Jonathan Edwards as he preached his unforgettable message, "Sinners in the Hands of an Angry God"? Would you have stomped out of the service as other people were screaming out in agony? (I'm pretty sure you wouldn't have liked it.)

The sobering thought is that God would never be angry toward men like Seymour and Edwards. He would never say acidly, " 'Sinners in the Hands of an Angry God'? Get real, Edwards." No, *you* get real, brother! What would you have done with the great Cane Ridge Revival? Yes, the power of God came down there just like it does in Brownsville and other places today! Would you have joined the drunken maniacs on horses who rode through the woods at breakneck speed trying to break up the crowd? The Holy Ghost threw those men off their horses and knocked them senseless! Some of them lay on the ground for days. If you are afraid of confrontation and change, that might have been you. Your rejection of the Spirit's work makes a mockery of the things of God.

Right now across America, groups of pastors and church denominational leaders are openly mocking the move of God across the nation! If you haven't noticed, God mockers tend to hang out with other God mockers. They not only hang out with their own kind, but they will even feed on *one another* like spiritual carnivores. Once they find a likely body for prey, they will happily gather in circles like buzzards to eat it.

These God mockers are writing "position papers" about external physical manifestations while totally ignoring the deeper work of God that is saving hundreds of thousands of souls and permanently changing lives. They pompously declare, "Well, that isn't God," and sign declarations of mockery for "distribution to the brethren" for their "education" (the Bible calls this sowing discord), while many of their church congregations continue to dwindle year after year.

Ask them about Acts 9:3-4, where God struck Paul to the ground on the road to Damascus, and they will pull out the same stock answer they've used to dismiss most of the Book of Acts and nearly all of the Epistles: "Oh, that was an *isolated incident*. Yeah, Paul fell under the power of God, *but that was back then. This is now.* This is not God."

Ask them about Jeremiah 23:9, where the prophet says, "...all my bones shake; I am like a drunken man, and like a man whom wine hath overcome, because of the Lord, and because of the words of His holiness." The God mockers will reply, "That was an isolated case too."

Ask about John 18:6 and the legion of soldiers who were struck to the ground when Jesus turned to meet them in Gethsemane. You will again hear the tired refrain, "That was an isolated occurrence." What about the great Wesleyan revival that birthed the fiery Methodist movement? What about the ministry of George White-field? He testified that the power of God came down and that people fell to the ground in his evangelistic campaigns. (By the way, many were struck by the convicting power of the Spirit of God, something which has become common in modern day revival meetings.) "Well, they were...uh, that was a delusion too. Besides, that was an isolated incident."

God mockers have much to fear. God will recall every curse uttered against His revival. He will replay every blasphemy whispered about the young people who were saved—the ones you declared would never last. He will remember every word spoken against the weary pastors who were refreshed by His Spirit under your disapproving gaze. To your shock and dismay, He will say in that day, "You were mocking Me! Yes, it was Me all along."

If you call yourself a Christian, take care how you bear the name of your Savior. Napoleon had a man in his army whose name was also Napoleon. However, this man was a coward. Napoleon went up to him and bluntly delivered an ultimatum: "Change your name, or live up to it!" That is what I have been commissioned to say to you:

Christian, Change Your Name, or Live Up to It!

This message has been preached in all different ways for centuries. A century ago, James Hastings wrote:

"God is mocked when we pretend to be His while we cut our being in two and give the better half to Satan, when we draw nigh unto Him with our lips while our hearts are far from Him, when we say 'I go, Sir,' and we go not, when we try to combine the vile pleasures of sin with the perfect allegiance which God requires, when we say, 'Lord, Lord' and we do evil continually."[1]

God mockers reap according to what they have sown. Long before we bring in the "final harvest," we reap from what we have done in this life, whether it be good or bad. Ask any alcoholic. The final judgment has not yet arrived, but he will tell you he has already found himself stuck in a field of thorns and briars, the fruit of his labor.

Look across this nation at the God mockers. They are already receiving some fruits of their labors. Friends, you will reap what you sow. Ask any backslider. Judgment Day has not yet come, but there is no peace in his life. Backsliders are reaping confusion, an unsettled spirit, and a perpetual lack of joy. We reap what we sow. That is why I tell folks, "Listen, if you're backslidden, don't call yourself a Christian because you're mocking the cross with the hypocrisy in your life."

God mockers have disturbed and confused this country. Most unsaved folks are trying their best to find *somebody* who really lives for God. If they could just find one person who lives holy and practices what they preach, they would have a standard, and they would get on fire for God too! However, all they find is a mockery.

Now for the good news: The law of reaping and sowing has a good side too. If you sow good seed, then you reap a good harvest. Nicholas von Zinzendorf led the great Moravian revival and reform movement in the 1700's. (If you want to read a story about a powerful move of God, read about the Moravian Missionary Alliance.) When Zinzendorf was a teenager, he united his school friends in a club he called "The Order of the Grain of Mustard Seed." Every member of the club received a ring inscribed with this motto: "No man liveth unto himself." These were just young lads! At a very young age, Zinzendorf was already planting the seeds of revival and holiness in his teenage friends. They constantly reminded one another, "You don't belong to yourself. Jesus has a plan for your life. You'll go where He wants you to go, won't you?"

Zinzendorf planted these seeds at a young age, and they produced a harvest in the great Moravian Missionary Brotherhood with branches extending throughout the world. Robert Murray McCheyne wept as he watched a group of Moravian missionaries dedicate themselves to a difficult mission field. They were going into a leper colony to preach the gospel, knowing full well that once they went in, they could never return. Maybe he heard one say, "Good-bye honey, I'll see you in Heaven. Good-bye son. I love you. I love you, daughter. Live for Jesus. Daddy needs to lead these lepers. You know I can't ever come back."

They were locked in for life and every one of them died in that leper colony. How could they make such a painful sacrifice for the sake of the gospel? Perhaps the seeds of greatness were planted in their youth—through "The Order of the Grain of Mustard Seed." They knew from their youth that "no man liveth unto himself." By the time they had come of age physically, those seeds of obedience and greatness had grown to maturity. The Moravians also had a profound effect on John Wesley, the founder of the Methodist movement. His writings describe how he went to one of their prayer meetings and had his life turned around.

The most important thing I have to say to a God mocker is this: You can repent and be forgiven. I am very concerned about your welfare. I have no doubts about your ability to share all the pertinent points of your doctrine, your theology, and your rules of church order. The problem comes when I ask if you know Christ, and if you are living a Christlike life. If your life is a standing mockery of Christ and the cross, then I am worried about you.

God mockers profess Christ's name with their lips, but their lives expose the fact that in their hearts, they believe that it's all just worthless. It is too late to tell me God doesn't deliver sinners—*He has already delivered me.* Once you know the truth, no lie will do. I like what one man (an alcoholic who encountered the living Christ) said when he was being water baptized at the Brownsville Revival, "I didn't need a 12-step program. It's a one-step." Jesus is the ultimate one-step, one-man deliverance program.

Even a God mocker can repent and be forgiven! Saul of Tarsus was a master mocker and a blatant religious scorner. Saul dramatically discovered that God will go out of His way to get hold of a mocker. Another God mocker, according to the Scriptures, was only a few feet away from Jesus in his last hours on earth: "The thieves also, which were crucified with Him, cast the same [insults] in His teeth" (Mt. 27:44). Both of those convicted criminals who were crucified beside Jesus joined in with the crowd who was mocking Jesus even though they shared His sentence of death! What a picture.

I think that Luke (or the witnesses he talked with) was a few feet closer to the cross than Matthew. He reports some things that no one else saw or heard. Luke must have heard Jesus say, "Father, forgive them; for they know not what they do" (Lk. 23:34a). I think he saw one of the God mockers being crucified with Jesus on Golgotha suddenly have a change of heart:

But the other answering rebuked him, saying, Dost not thou fear God, seeing thou art in the same condemnation? And we indeed justly; for we receive the due reward of our deeds: but this man hath done nothing amiss (Luke 23:40-41).

Luke says this repentant God mocker and thief turned to Jesus and said, "Lord, remember me." I believe Luke was close enough to see this transaction and tell us, "And he said unto Jesus, Lord, remember me when Thou comest into Thy kingdom" (Lk. 23:42). I'm telling you mockers can receive forgiveness. Luke tells us, "And Jesus said unto him, Verily I say unto thee, Today shalt thou be with Me in paradise" (Lk. 23:43). Hallelujah!

Don't say, "That was an isolated case." The Bible record is good enough for me. How could someone who was hurling abuses at God one moment float on angels' wings to paradise with Jesus a few minutes later? There is only one answer: *He repented.*

Are You Committing Mayhem?

I may lose a few readers at this point, but I know that I will stand alone before the Great Judge on Judgment Day. Although the superintendent of the Assemblies of God and the pastor of Brownsville Assembly agree with me and support me daily, they won't be able to stand with me before the Great Judge. I'll stand alone, and *you will stand alone before Him too*. You will stand alone to answer for every seed of disunity and discord you have sown among the brethren, for every occasion you *cursed another man's ministry*. No one will be able to stand there for you—you will be all by your lonesome, friend. You may hear the Almighty say: "Why did you mock Me and

My Spirit's work in front of your friends when I moved through another church on the other side of your city? Why did you rip My name and My people to shreds?"

Whether you are a pastor, a teenager, or a seminary professor, I am warning you: One day we will each stand before God to answer for our words, our attitudes, and our works. Have you committed spiritual mayhem? *Mayhem* is "the shredding apart, the ripping apart of a body." You have committed spiritual mayhem if you have seen the hand of the Lord on a part of the Blood-washed Body of Christ, and in your disapproval, you have reached up and ripped off the whole arm or limb with your mocking words of criticism, condemnation, and rejection. That is spiritual mayhem. The sad truth is that all God is doing in this revival is saving a few souls in just a little different way from the methods you have used in the past. *Beware of the damning powers of mockery.*

During a recent Friday night revival service, five gentlemen entered the sanctuary at Brownsville Assembly of God and carefully positioned themselves. One man went to each of the four corners of the room, and the fifth man settled down in the middle. He was there so he could give signals to the others. The men were from another church in Pensacola— one that basically believes that everyone else is wrong but them. They came to the revival with one purpose in mind: to ridicule the move of God. I was amazed when I realized that those five men sat unmoved while we heard some of the most amazing testimonies of changed lives ever heard during our Friday night baptismal services. How can a true God lover sit unmoved when God is so powerfully glorified through the changed lives of sinners washed in the Blood of the Lamb?

Then these men sat through my message on "Mistaken Identity," which is based on the Lord's rebuke of those who claim to have done many great things in His name thinking they were right when they were dead wrong. They sat through all of that untouched and unmoved—even though that particular night I preached out of the King James Bible (the only Bible these men will ever use—they believe any other Bible translation is of the devil).

All night long, these men were seething and frothing at the mouth like ravenous lions waiting to kill something. Finally, I gave the altar call and hundreds and hundreds of searching souls came forward, weeping and wailing and crying out to God. Even that didn't satisfy these men. They had entered God's house with a verdict already pronounced in their hearts. They were still mocking. Almost 1,000 people came forward to the altars that night, yet these five men were still mocking God. They didn't realize that they weren't mocking Brownsville, they were dealing with something and Someone a whole lot bigger than Brownsville Assembly of God.

We normally never give the time of day to critics or accusers, but it is important for you to see how these men were deceived. As the ministry around the altar progressed, the men stood up and began to walk around the crowded building with tracts in their hands. Every time they came upon someone who had been touched by the Holy Ghost and was on the floor receiving from God—these men dropped their tracts on top of them. They wrote on the tract, "Look at yourself. You're making a fool out of yourself. Get saved." Every tract had directions to their church on it as well. I'm telling you, friend, it was a mockery. They forgot one very important fact:

God was moving in the house. The Bible says, "Touch not Mine anointed, and do My prophets no harm" (Ps. 105:15). That is a deadly warning to every God mocker on this planet.

The very next night, I felt led to reveal the rest of the story. I told this story to the congregation and to the television audience and then I said:

> "God is in the house tonight too. As a matter of fact, there is somebody in this room from that church tonight—I can feel you right now. And if you say a word right now, you are going to be ushered out.

> "What you didn't know, sir, was that on Friday night when you came up to the platform and made a threat on my life, God was on to you. You said, 'We're going to remove that man,' speaking of me. And you said that to an undercover cop! There are police officers all through this place. You can't tell, can you? They're everywhere. Yes, you uttered your threat to a policeman.

> "Did you know, sir, that within a few minutes after you gave him your name and a false address, he had your name, your real address, where you work, who you live with, what you drive, and what you make—he knew everything about you, friend. Do you want to know something? That was just proof to me: *You can't mock Him.* Be not deceived. God is not mocked. Whatsoever a man sows, that shall he also reap!"

Be careful, God mocker. Do you know who you are messing with? You're not messing with Steve Hill. You're not messing with John Kilpatrick or the Assemblies of God. You're not messing with the Baptists, or the

Methodists. You are messing with God Almighty. When He moves, you had better back off.

God is after revival, and nothing is going to stop Him. It is God who sends revival. He is the Supreme Source of the river of His glory. He alone commands, "Deeper, *now!*" and watches the river flow deeper. He is the one who says, "Houston, Texas—*now!*" He is the one who says, "Toronto, Canada—*now!*" He is the one who says, "Australia—*now!*"

My friend, the Blood of Jesus is about to wash the vilest sinners clean somewhere in a revival service today, whether you and I like it or not. Be not deceived. God is not mocked. Whatsoever things you sow, you shall reap. I challenge you, friend: Sow some good seed today. Isn't it time for a change? Whether you are away from God, backslidden, or if your life simply does not fit that word *Christian*, you still need to change. If you call yourself a Christian but your eyes are glued to vile pornographic movies, if you allow your heart to be infatuated with another even though you are married, if you allow yourself to be consumed with the poison of alcohol and drugs, it is a mockery. If you are consumed with sin in any form and still call yourself a Christian, it is a mockery, friend. You need to repent. If you do, there is hope.

Is there something in your life that is separating you from God? This is your chance to repent and turn that mess around. You probably already know it's an abomination, but there is a chance that you have been deceived. Don't tell yourself, "Everything is going to be all right. It's going to take care of itself, Brother Steve." It won't.

God has one answer for you: "Be not deceived. God is not mocked." This is your opportunity to get right with God right now. He isn't interested in your ideas about religion or the doctrines of your church. He is going to say, "I spoke to you the day you read *The God Mockers*. You heard the truth, now what fruit do you have to show for it? Do you really know Me, or do you just use My name for your own purposes?"

Only one thing really matters. You can go to hell with baptismal waters on your face and a confirmation certificate hanging on the wall behind your desk. You can go to hell even though you were the most faithful Sunday school teacher in your denomination and a founding member of the largest church in the city! Answer this question: *Do you know Jesus?*

Do you wake up in the morning with Jesus on your heart? Do you go to sleep at night with Jesus on your heart? Do you eat, drink, and breathe Jesus? If not, then I need to tell you something—you are not exempt. You can't hide behind four walls because God is coming to your house and into your bedroom to confront you. This isn't about Methodism or Pentecostalism. It's not about a church; it's about Jesus. Do you know Him? Get on your face before God and ask Him to forgive you for your stinking religious attitudes and your mockery of the things of God. Drop to your knees before God and say, "Jesus, I need You. Forgive me, Lord."

God is putting an exclamation point on this. He's saying to you, "Get right with Me right now." This may be your last moment's breath. I've known of people walking out of a revival meeting and dying two hours later. Some of those who died suddenly were saved in those meetings, but others left this world and entered eternity with a bitter curse on their lips. What will you say today?

I want you to pray a simple prayer out loud with me right now. It will seal what God is doing in your heart:

Dear Jesus, thank You for speaking to me. Today, Jesus, I refuse to mock You. I refuse to be a mockery. I want to bring You praise, glory, and honor today. I ask You to forgive me because I have sinned against You and I have hurt You and others. Forgive me, Jesus. Wash my sins away. I repent. I ask You to be my Savior, my Lord, and my very best friend. I commit myself to You 100 percent. From this moment on, You can count on me, Jesus. I will be a loyal, learning follower. In Your precious name I pray, Lord Jesus. Amen.

Endnote

1. James Hastings, D.D., *The Great Texts of the Bible* (Edinburgh: T.&T. Clark, 1913), p. 439.

Chapter 2

The Sin Mockers

You might be saved already, but whether you are a drug-addicted teenager or a fame-addicted TV preacher, the bottom line of God's anointing is *repentance*. The Bible says, "Follow...holiness, without which no man shall see the Lord" (Heb. 12:14). Without holiness, pastor, there will be no miracles. Without holiness, evangelist, you might see change and be deceived, because you know you can get drunk, preach the Word, and still watch people get saved. We've seen sin mixed with ministry for centuries (usually at great cost to the Church). But, friend, without the anointing, without holiness, nothing will happen in *America*. Nothing will happen in our nation or in our churches unless we get rid of the sin in our lives!

You may be totally ignorant about what I'm talking about, even though you've gone to church services and revival meetings where people praise God and jump up and down in joy. The problem is that the bottom line of all your troubles is *sin*, and you must allow Jesus Christ to deal with your sin before you can be saved. God never intended for you to carry the weight of your sin in your life. He never intended for you to be driven by pornography, chemical addictions, or illicit sexual desires; yet people always act like He has. They come up to me constantly and say, "Well, I can quit this. I can quit that. I'm in charge of my life, not my problems."

Most of these people don't like it when I call their bluff and ask, "If you can quit all on your own, then why don't you?" They usually answer, "Well, I don't want to," but I come right back and say, "Oh yes you do—you just can't." The problem is called *sin*, and it was ingrained in you and me from the moment we were born. The truth is, according to God's Word you were born into sin and the only one who can set you free is Jesus Christ.

"Fools make a mock at sin" (Prov. 14:9a). A fool is a man or a woman who is stupid. A fool is a silly, giddy person, a person who lacks sense or judgment. The Book of Proverbs covers every aspect of the fool. If you want to find out if you're a fool, read Proverbs. It hurts. I'll never forget the Scripture that says, "Even a fool is counted wise when he keeps his mouth shut" (see Prov. 17:28). Have you ever opened your mouth and then wished you hadn't? It's best to keep it shut because no one will ever know your status one way or the other. (But as soon as you open your mouth, you might prove you're a fool.) To *mock* means "to scoff at, to treat with contempt, to ridicule, to make sport of, to mimic." Fools make a mock at sin. They take sin lightly.

Jesus Christ did not take sin lightly. He took sin seriously—all the way to the cross where He died to *take away the sin of the world* (see Jn. 1:29). The Son of God died to set you free from your sin. That should tell you that if you're taking sin lightly, you are a fool. I didn't write this book to make anybody happy. This is one of those messages that makes spiritual babies cry, but I have to preach the Word.

What do I mean by "sin"? My definition of sin is "anything that Jesus wouldn't do." Is that clear enough? Fools don't take the work of the cross seriously because they don't take sin seriously. This leads me to my first point: *A fool treats sin lightly because he is so accustomed to it.* If you believe a lie long enough, it will finally appear to be the truth to you. The same thing goes for habits and sin. If you commit a sin long enough, it will finally begin to sear your conscience and warp your idea of right and wrong.

Pornography is one of the most prevalent sins ruining America today. The Internet has made hard-core pornography available free of charge to anyone who can turn on a computer—whether the victim is 3 or 103 years old. I've ministered to people who were introduced to pornography as children. By the time they reached their early teens (still too young to be admitted to a triple-X rated porno theater), they were pulling the most grotesque stuff you can think of off the Internet. When they finally did feel a little guilt and have a change of heart, their idea of "right and wrong" was so warped that they thought they were "better" because they slipped back to "just reading *Playboy* magazines each month." They had become so accustomed to pornography that their conscience had become seared. Only the Blood of Jesus and the Word of God can fully cleanse these people.

Every day I meet people who give me the same old line: "I'm not *that bad!*" All they do is apply the line to whatever sin is gripping their lives: "I don't drink *like I used to.*" Have you ever heard that? When I say, "Oh, you mean you still drink?" they invariably answer, "Oh, yeah. I still drink. *I just don't drink like I used to.*" That is a mockery of sin. Are you taking sin lightly because you are accustomed to it?

What programs are you watching on HBO or through your local cable or satellite service? Would you want Jesus to sit down beside you and watch each of those programs with you tonight? How about those videotapes hidden away from the children and away from the church folks who visit you from time to time? Have you watched garbage for so long that you have become accustomed to it? That is because you take it lightly. Remember that mockery also refers to the act of looking at something like it is worthless and powerless. The devil will sit with you in your den by the hour saying, "This won't really damn your soul. It won't really take you to hell. After all, it's not really that bad." As you continue watching, you continue lusting. Continuing to do the sinful things you're doing, friend, is a sign of a sure fool.

I appreciate a true friend who will speak honestly with me. What kind of friend do you have? Do you have somebody who will cuddle up to you and say that everything is fine? Or do you have a friend who will come up to you in concern and say, "Listen, I really don't think you should be dating that guy." When you say, "That's none of your business," does she refuse to back off? Does she say, "Well, Susan, don't you know that Sam has been in bed with four other girls at the school? It's a common thing with him. As your friend, I just think that you're his next target"? If they are real friends, then they won't be surprised when you drag out the same old lie that has been around since the beginning: "No, he said he loves me. He said I'm different, I'm not like the other girls." True friends will keep on pressing the point until you either listen or want to dump them as friends. If you do, you will have just pushed God right out of your life.

True friends will ask you about your extended lunches with your private secretary, sir. Whether you are a pastor, a businessperson, or a doctor, good friends can save your hide by calling you to account in love. They will ask you about unusual friendships, business associations, and money transactions. They will probe to see why you have withdrawn from church activities or why you avoid godly friends every weekend. They will ask you why you constantly talk about the "action sequences" in so-called adult films, although you really don't want to admit that the scenes you remember best are the lewd sexual scenes. Godly friends are gifts from God because they have your best interests at heart. Thank the Lord for people like that. Thank God for people who will call sin, sin.

My second point is that *a fool makes a mockery of sin because it is often mixed with good*. It sometimes appears gray instead of black or white. The Bible says that satan is transformed into an angel of light, and that the people through whom he operates often have the *appearance* of "ministers of righteousness" (see 2 Cor. 11:14-15). Young person, the devil has been successfully deceiving people for thousands of years. He is the undisputed master of deception. The finest magicians and illusionists in the world couldn't begin to compare to him. He will woo you into sin little by little, by mixing a little flavoring with the poison.

Sin often appears attractive. The Bible says sin can be pleasurable—for a season (see Heb. 11:25). When a pond freezes over after a cold night, a young child can only see the thin veneer of ice. It all looks frozen and almost irresistible, so the child may walk out on the ice for some innocent fun—totally unaware that the surface veneer is disguising some dangerously thin ice patches that could take his life if he falls through! That is how sin is, friend. Sparkling water can be poisoned, and Halloween candy can be full of razor blades. Satan will oftentimes mix a little good with his bad just to entice you.

Ungodly relationships are masterminded by lucifer himself to entangle and destroy the righteous. Time and again I warn young Christian girls and women, "Don't fall for it when a man says, 'I believe in God.' Get real! Don't fall for it when he says, 'Sure, I'll go to church with you.' When he piously says grace over a meal, don't deceive yourself into saying, 'Boy, he seems to be a really good guy.' If you listen to the Spirit of God within you, you will know whether or not he's going after God." My friend, don't let the devil mix a little good in with his sin. He doesn't mind giving you some good stuff as long as he can hook you on the bad stuff.

All across America, Sunday morning church services are packed to capacity with a little bit of good. Satan doesn't mind the good stuff as long as he can keep out the hard-core preaching. He has to keep the people from hearing about the power of the Blood and the cross. He likes preachers who say, "I just make it user-friendly. As long as everybody is happy, that's all that matters." Careful, friend. These "joy churches" are full of heathens. They are right to say there is joy in the Christian faith, but joy only comes after the cross and the Blood have completed their work! Joy churches are filled with the 78 percent of Americans who believe they're going to Heaven even though many of them have never been to the cross. Satan will do everything he can to keep those people skating on the thin ice of the joy church. He doesn't want them to know that they won't go to Heaven if they haven't been to the cross. He doesn't want them to know that the cross is not a one-time visit. He hopes they never read the apostle Paul's statement: "I am crucified with Christ: nevertheless I live" (Gal. 2:20a). Friend, if you name the name of Jesus, then you are called to live on the cross.

My final point is this: *A fool makes light of sin because he is blinded to its consequences.* If you knew what that sin was really doing and where it was leading you, friend, you would never do it! What unmarried girl would crawl into bed with a man and commit fornication if she knew a baby would be born in nine months because of that sex act? I believe she would walk out of that bedroom. She would never do it if she *knew* she would get pregnant as a consequence of her sin. If she could see that man flying out of her life like a bird after using and abusing her, if she knew the consequences of that sin, she would never step foot in that bedroom!

Have you noticed that satan will never show you the consequences ahead of time? He will always remind you of the good and not the bad when it comes to sin. The Christian who used to hit the bar scene before he was saved will tell you that almost any time he passes a bar, he will see people out front laughing and giggling with cigarettes between their fingers. The girls (usually attractive) will have their arms around the guys, and they will all look like they are having a good time. What happens then? The believer's memories kick in. *Man, I remember that. It wasn't too long ago that I would get myself a couple drinks, find some women, and enjoy all that stuff.* If he doesn't consciously take those thoughts captive, out of his mind, they will dominate his thoughts long after the bar has disappeared from the rearview mirror and into the night.

Do you know what the devil will never do? He won't remind that man about what would usually happen later on in those evenings when he used to hug the toilet in the bar and vomit his guts out. Somehow that never makes it into the beer commercials and movies, and satan tries to see to it that it doesn't make it into our memories either. He never says, "Now, wait a minute. Don't you remember what happened later on that night? You puked your guts out, man." No, satan is a sly fox, friend. He won't remind you of that past relationship that ripped your life to shreds either. He'll say things like, "Well, that was just a freak thing. This time it will really work. It doesn't matter whether they are as religious as I am or not." Friend, don't fall for it.

A fool makes light of sin because he is blinded of its consequences. Sin will always flower over its consequences. Do you know why they have flowers at funerals? Walk into a church when someone is having a funeral, especially when the funeral is for somebody who was well-known. You can't even see the wall of the church for the flowers! It's beautiful. I think the wall should be black for death. Instead of having the people look at the wreaths and orchids and all of the pretty colors, I think they should see a wall of black and an arrow pointing to the body in a black casket—that's death.

The problem is that we don't want to talk about death. "Put flowers all over it, please. Don't make me think about it." Most graveside funeral services make you think you're in an outside concert hall with their ornate furnishings, flowers, and nice carpets rolled out. Take up the carpet, friend. Do everyone a favor and let reality have its way. There is cold earth underneath those carpets. There is a hole that is six feet deep hidden somewhere under the magic show created by the funeral parlor. Look past the nice little brass ring and the fancy crank mechanisms used to lower the casket after everybody leaves. Friend, walk over there and look into the hole: That is where you are going.

The devil will cover up the consequences of sin, but I don't care what it looks like. The teenage boy who died in a high-speed car accident was drunk out of his mind. He's not in that casket anymore; he's standing before God Almighty. The Bible says, "...it is appointed unto men once to die, but after this the judgment" (Heb. 9:27). Death and judgment are the consequences of sin, and fools don't like to think about it. They would rather make a mockery of it all. The last laugh is on them.

Sin will say to you, "It may happen to other people, but it will never happen to you. You won't get pregnant. You won't get hooked. You won't get caught." That's a lie, friend. Sin will destroy you. Don't be a fool. If there is sin in your life, you can be sure that lucifer is the driving force behind it. He's driving you, friend. You are being driven like a madman to the edge of oblivion. That's what satan does best. He is a master of deception and destruction because he has been practicing his dark craft for thousands of years. He knows your heart, and he may decide to use the same tactic he used on David thousands of years ago. Perhaps he will try to entice you into sin by getting you to lag behind so you will end up in the wrong place at the wrong time with a modern-day Bathsheba. He knew Samson's weakness and he knows yours. He knew Peter's weakness. Where are you supposed to be today? Are you lingering behind with the wrong friends and associates?

Sin will satisfy you only until it has sunk its claws deep down into your soul. Its evil will grip you and rip you. Sin will caress your hand, kiss you on the cheek, and whisper empty promises into your love-struck ear. It will woo you into its bedchamber, lull you to sleep, and then stab you in the back. It will promise you everything and leave you with nothing. Sin will promise you heaven on earth and give you eternity in hell. It will love you for a season and curse you for eternity. Don't be a fool. Don't make a mockery of sin. If there is sin in your life, you need to come clean just like I did decades ago. Don't be a fool.

Don't classify sin mockers as "those people" who utter blasphemies and mock God's Word. Don't say to yourself, "I hope some young people will get saved through this book. They need to get the sin out of their lives." Listen my friend, what is coming out of *your* mouth? What did you do with *your* day? How much like Christ are you? Where do you stand with Jesus this moment?

I recently led an 87-year-old man to the Lord during the revival. It would have been easy for him to stand around saying, "Well, I hope the young people get saved—this generation needs God." But the truth is, *you* need God. Is there sin in your life? What good is it if you lived on fire for Jesus 50 years, and then the last ten years of your life, you lived a bitter, angry, critical life? Don't you think Jesus is going to judge that?

Have you been taking sin lightly? If so, the Bible calls you a fool, and no one likes to be called a fool. Fools make a mockery of sin because they take it lightly. They don't see the pain it can cause. It put Jesus on the cross, and that's enough for you to come clean and get right with God.

Perhaps you have gone through a heartache, and you are now turning to God. It is time to turn that heartache around. Stop blaming everything on the past. You pop pills into your body to get up, and pills to go to sleep at night to cover the pain of a traumatic experience from long ago. Friend, it's over. It is time to get a grip on life. Come clean and get the sin out of your life so you can go on with God. Satan is playing havoc with your life. Don't be a fool. Don't fall for it.

If you are religious but have to admit that you don't know Jesus, then I want you to pay close attention: Religion will damn your soul. Religion is hanging around the cross, but true Christianity is getting on the cross. Religion is doing all the right things and not knowing Him. Do you know Him? Do you wake up in the morning with Jesus on your heart? Do you go to sleep at night with Jesus on your heart? Do you eat, drink, and breathe Jesus? If you don't, then I must warn you that Jesus Christ is coming back for a spotless Bride. Your garments have been touched by sin. There are stains all over them, and you don't look like a Bride.

I went to a store the other day with my wife, Jeri. We wanted to pick up a framed picture, and I did what I shouldn't do. I let her go in by herself. I parked outside in the parking lot and kept the motor running. I literally watched the needle go down, friend. After about 45 minutes, I thought, *Now we were going to get just one framed picture, right? It's a small shop. They don't sell anything but frames*. Finally Jeri came back to the car, sometime before the needle passed the "E" on the gauge and said, "Sorry, Steve, but the woman didn't know Jesus."

I said, "What?" and Jeri replied, "She's been divorced four times. She's had all kinds of heartache in her life. Steve, I had to do it. I just had to spend time with her." That is a picture of Christians in real life—Jesus is on their lips. When they walk into a place, they scope it out in their spirits: "Picture frame, okay. That's what I came for, but what did *You* bring me here for, Jesus?" That is the way Christians live. If you don't live that way, friend, then you're not carrying the burden of the Lord, because He came for sinners.

If you are reading these words and there is sin in your life, or if you don't know the Lord, you can meet Jesus Christ and experience total freedom right now. You may be a very religious person—a Buddhist, a Muslim, a Jew, a cult member, a witch or a warlock—but God says you are going to hell if you haven't repented of your sin and received Jesus Christ as your Lord and Savior. Those aren't my words—they come directly from the Word of God. You need to step away from the sin that binds you. The moment you repent and ask Him in, Heaven looks down, hell looks up, and the chains binding your life snap! I've watched it happen in millions of hearts over the last few years.

If you are serious about receiving forgiveness, then I want you to pray this prayer with me right now. Don't delay or hesitate. Don't hesitate and say you'll do it tomorrow. The only thing holding you back is a demonic characteristic called pride. God abhors and despises it. God says, "But to this one I will look, to him who is humble, contrite in spirit, and who trembles at My word" (Is. 66:2b NAS). Pray this prayer out loud, no matter where you are. Bold requests require bold commitment:

Dear Jesus, Thank You for speaking to me through this chapter. I refuse to be a sin mocker. I refuse to make a mockery of sin, and I refuse to be called a fool. I want to be called a child of God; I want to be called a Christian and then live up to that holy name. I ask You to forgive me for my sins—I've hurt You and I've hurt others, and I repent of my sins. Please forgive me and make me clean in Your sight through the Blood of Jesus. I ask You to become my Savior and Lord right now, and I commit my life to You. Thank You for loving me so much. In Jesus' name I thank You, Father. Amen.

Chapter 3

Check the Tree!

I will never forget the time we were dealing with some teenagers in a Christ-centered drug rehabilitation program. One particular young man in our program was on fire for God, but his father used to drive by in front of our house and curse us!

The father and his son were from a very wealthy family in the city. He hated us because his son had become a Christian and broke free from his drug addiction through our program. He was ablaze for Jesus Christ. This man could handle his son being hooked on drugs, but he couldn't accept him as a Christian. His hatred was so deep that he used to bitterly curse us at the top of his lungs while driving by our ministry house. No matter how hard we tried to make peace with him, he just got worse and worse. He did everything he could to come against us.

Early one morning, our program director was reading the Word of God when he was led to the verse that says, "But the Lord is with me as a mighty terrible one: therefore my persecutors shall stumble, and they shall not prevail" (Jer. 20:11a). It was four o'clock in the morning when he saw this verse, and he immediately knew it was for the man who cursed them day after day. He didn't pray that it would happen, and he didn't rejoice; in fact, he was sorry for the man who was so unyielding in his hatred and unreasoning opposition to God's work.

Five hours later, at nine o'clock, the man who had opposed our work for God fell down two flights of stairs and broke his neck instantly. He was pronounced dead where he lay at the bottom of the stairs. Every time I remember this incident, I am reminded that the same God who warned kings and nations, "Touch not Mine anointed, and do My prophets no harm" (Ps. 105:15), is still alive and well in our day. Whether or not you believe that God took that man out of the way, you have to acknowledge that all of us will stand before Him one day and give an account of all that we believed, rejected, and did in this life.

The more that I read the Word, the more I am convinced that the preaching of John the Baptist, Paul, Peter, and Jesus Christ contained truths that modern preachers avoid. It makes me think, *Dear God, we've only given half the message! The other half is something that is about to happen.* I'm afraid that it isn't going to be as sweet as the first half. America knows I'm right, because most Americans know in their gut that they are racing toward judgment.

The Lord recently woke me up from a sound sleep, and I felt an urgency emanating from the voice of Jesus, *a warning that time itself was no longer on our side.* The grains of sand, my friend, are at the base of the funnel in the eternal hourglass. Only a few moments remain. The hands on the clock are moving toward midnight and the curtains of this major production we call life are about to close upon the last scene. There will be no encore. There will be no second opportunity. The play will soon be over. Only moments remain for many of us to write the very last act in our lives.

It is time to pay close attention to the voice of God. Too many of us have squandered most of our days in the past year in selfish pleasures and pursuits. Nothing was done to advance toward Christ, so precious souls continued to deteriorate in sin rather than exert domination over sin. Ask yourself, "Did I seize every opportunity to go after God, or did I laze away the days, drifting aimlessly and hopelessly away from Heaven's peaceful harbor?" Whatever you do, don't tell yourself, "Well, this doesn't apply to me." This word isn't just for Billy, or Susan, or Diane—it is for *you!* Judgment is coming to America, but judgment always knocks first at the House of God!

> *For the time is come that judgment must begin at the house of God: and if it first begin at us, what shall the end be of them that obey not the gospel of God? And if the righteous scarcely be saved, where shall the ungodly and the sinner appear?* (1 Peter 4:17-18)

This is a clarion call. Today you will be summoned and held accountable for your choices. This is an arraignment in which you answer to the Judge concerning the charges leveled against you. It is a "pop quiz" of the most dreaded kind. It is like brushing up to the edge of hell, peering in, feeling the fervent heat of the flames, but not yet falling in headlong. It's like standing in a holding cell knowing that in a few minutes, you will face the right arm of the law in a life-or-death decision of guilt or innocence. It is time to think about your destiny. Are you ready to give all to the Lord?

Times of judgment are times of godly fear, self-examination, and serious contemplation. The good news is that when you are found guilty (and you will be), there is hope. Only one Advocate is qualified to take your case before the Father because He alone was willing to pay the price to set you free. You had better let Jesus stand in for you before the Judge.

The Lord has been extremely patient toward you and many others up to this point, but even His patience will wear thin. He has cared for you. Now it's time for you to care for Him. He gave up all of Heaven and made His way to the world for you. It's time for you to give up all the world and make your way toward Heaven for Him. He has called unto you. Now it's time for you to call unto Him. Time is running out. Just as the sun rises to bring us a new day, don't forget, friend, it also sets, ushering in a cloak of darkness. Just as there has been a dispensation of grace and mercy, there is coming a time, a season of judgment and wrath.

"I have blessed you," saith the Lord. "Now it's time for you to bless Me. I've given you My life. Now it's time for you to give Me yours. I've fulfilled My part. Now it's time for you to fulfill yours. I walked on the earth for you. Now it's time for you to walk on the earth for Me. I have called unto you. Now it's time for you to call unto Me."

There were present at that season some that told Him of the Galileans, whose blood Pilate had mingled with their sacrifices. And Jesus answering said unto them, Suppose ye that these Galileans were sinners above all *the Galileans, because they suffered such things? I tell you, Nay: but, **except ye repent, ye shall all likewise perish**. Or those eighteen, upon whom the tower in Siloam fell, and slew them, think ye that they were sinners above all men that dwelt in Jerusalem? I tell you, Nay: but, **except ye repent, ye shall all likewise perish*** (Luke 13:1-5).

Jesus said these things, so don't get upset at me. Too many of us like "Twinkie" messages filled with sweet bread, sugar, and cream. Like spoiled children, we constantly demand an unhealthy and unbalanced diet of God's Word, but we need the whole counsel of God. Jesus our Savior often "filleted" religious hypocrites alive! He loved the children of the people of that day, prayed for their sick, and even raised their dead; but there came a time when He told them, "Drink My Blood. Eat My flesh, or get out of My face" (see Jn. 6:53-66).

After Jesus told the people they needed to repent, He told them a parable to help them understand just how serious His Father was about obedience:

...A certain man had a fig tree planted in his vineyard; and he came and sought fruit thereon, and found none. Then said he unto the dresser of his vineyard, Behold, these three years I come seeking fruit on this fig tree, and find none: cut it down; why cumbereth it [why does it use up] *the ground? And he answering said unto him, Lord, let it alone this year also, till I shall dig about it, and dung it: and if it bear fruit, well; and if not, then after that thou shalt cut it down* (Luke 13:6-9).

My friend: *Check the tree.* Just before He told this parable Jesus said we have to repent or perish. We could view the fig tree as the Jewish nation, the vineyard as the

Church, the owner of the vineyard as God, and the vine-dresser as Christ. Another interpretation would see Christ as the owner and the Holy Spirit as the vinedresser.

This parable has universal application, so I'm going to make it simple: *You are the fig tree.* The vineyard is the earth, the place God has planted you. The owner of the vineyard is God, and the vinedresser is Christ. This puts us in a difficult situation, because we are held account-able for our choices and our actions. All of a sudden, a "ticket to Heaven" just isn't enough to please God. He wants to see some return on His costly investment.

Number 1: You were planted on this planet for a purpose.

If you were planted on this planet for a purpose, can you get away with living like you weren't? Stay with me, friend. You didn't even pick up this book by chance— God brought you and I together to help us fulfill our di-vine purpose. God put you on this earth for a purpose, and that does *not* mean He put you here just to make money and satisfy all your carnal delights. He did not put you here just so you could become socially popular and surround yourself with friends and admirers. He did not put you here just so you can climb some corporate or political ladder and run a factory or branch of government.

God did not put you here just so you could become the most benevolent man on earth, organize charity drives and telethons, and give untold millions to the less fortunate of the world. Yes, these things are wonderful, but you were planted on this planet for one primary rea-son above all others: to bear fruit for God and to have fellowship with Him. (And you are doomed to be miser-able if you're not doing it.)

Drug addicts know what I mean by being miserable. They know that you can pump in the morphine, the crystal meth, the crack cocaine, and the heroin. You can fill your veins with it and you will get a cheap thrill. They will also tell you that it comes and goes like the wind, leaving you aching even more for the next cheap thrill. Nothing satisfies. You might satisfy yourself for a few moments with a fling with another sex partner, but any adulterer and fornicator will tell you that it's all over in a heartbeat. You'll just wake up the next day empty.

On the other hand, when you get in fellowship with the God who created you, it's like nothing else in the world. There is nothing like waking up every morning full of joy and anticipation and saying, "This is the day that the Lord has made; I will rejoice and be glad in it. Good morning, Holy Ghost. Good morning, Jesus. Good morning, Father. Where are we going today?"

What kind of fruit does the Lord seek? He wants to see the fruit of repentance, praise, thanksgiving, but He isn't getting it. God has an even greater right to pick the fruit that comes from your tree than does the Georgia peach farmer who harvests fruit from his own orchard. After all, He prepared the soil, planted you, pruned you, sprayed you, and watered you from the beginning. On top of everything else, He died for you and gave you eternal life. He gets the fruit. He brought you into this world, He nursed you, He put people around you to change your filthy diapers, and He took care of you. When you were dying of one disease or problem after another, He nursed you back to health. Yet when we "turn 18" (spiritually speaking), bless God, we say, "Now I have control of the reins!" Friend, you never did and you never will. He did it all! It's all God!

Number 2: God expects to find fruit in your life.

This may send a jolt of adrenaline into your system, but God is checking your tree for fruit. For years now, God has been expecting to receive a harvest in your life. God is looking for fruit—how long has He been disappointed?

The fig tree in Palestine is a tree that is full of foliage. There are so many leaves that they can create a deep shade even during the hot Israeli summer. If you go over there in the summer, even then you will find people sitting under the fig trees. Jesus mentioned seeing Nathanael sitting under a fig tree in John 1:47-48. When Jesus told the parable of the fig tree, He wasn't praising the tree for its leaves and its ability to provide shade to people on a hot day. That was nice, but it wasn't its central purpose for existence. I want to tell you something, friend. God did not put you on this planet to produce leaves.

God is searching the face of the earth like He did during the days of Noah, and He is looking for *fruit*. Do you know what He sees? Leaves. That is all God sees in the so-called Church today—leaves. God could care less about leaves, friend. He doesn't want leaves. Jesus said His Father wants fruit. Meanwhile, most of us in the church are so religious that we are laden down with leaves. We walk by one another and say, "My, you sure can sing. Just look at those leaves!" or "Boy, you can preach up a storm! I sure admire your leaves," or "You're a good man. You are such a good provider for the family. You have a fine crop of leaves on your tree," or "You are a good mother. Nobody does it like you do. You sure take good care of your kids. Anybody would be impressed with your leaves."

God is sick and tired of leaves—He wants to see fruit! Take your leaves and leave. He is sick of them. Take them all.

There's not a peach farmer in Georgia who would be satisfied just to see leaves. He can't go down to the market and shout, "Leaves! Leaves! Fresh ripe leaves! Fresh fuzzy leaves!" No, people want peaches. They want fruit according to the variety of the fruit tree. They want to sink their teeth into a succulent peach, a fresh, crisp apple, or a juicy sweet orange. You eat fruit; you burn leaves. What are you giving God through your life: bushels of fruit or piles of worthless leaves? Have you produced anything worthwhile this year? If nothing is coming out of your life, then Jesus says God is sick of it!

The owner of the vineyard in Jesus' parable expected a harvest in due season. God expects a harvest from *you* in due season too. How many harvest seasons have come and gone without fruit in your life? Time after time, frustrated parents have come to me in this revival. They are frustrated with the fruitless lives of their children. One mother told me recently: "My daughter is 18 years old. We took care of her, nursed her, watched over her, fed her, and then we got her a car on her 16th birthday. Then she just left home to live with some 37-year-old man." They just wanted to see a little fruit, some type of maturity to come from all their labor with their daughter. All they got was leaves.

Other parents are living out the parable of the barren fig tree. They tell me, "I'm sick of him. He's my son and I love him, but the doors are locked. We've chained the door and changed the locks. He is not permitted in our house anymore until we see real change." Then I've had kids come to me and say, "Do you know what my parents did? They locked me out of my own house!" I tell them,

"Number one, it's not your house. How old are you?" "I'm 21." "Go find your own place to live." "Yeah, but it costs a lot of money." "Now, you're getting the idea. Now, you're beginning to understand what life is really like out there. Do you have a job? Good. What are you making?" "$4.75 an hour." "You can't get much with that, can you? You appreciate a full refrigerator now, don't you?"

If as parents, we are looking for fruit in our kids, how much more is God looking for fruit from you and me? As a parent, I want people to come up and say, "Steve, your son Ryan is such a God lover. He's so helpful and kind. He always does so much for everyone else." I want to see fruit and more fruit. God wants the same thing.

Has God been waiting a long time for you? He is patient, but according to the Scripture, even His patience has limits. The fig tree bears fruit three times a year— early spring, summer, and autumn. The owner of the vineyard in the Lord's parable had been waiting patiently for fruit for three years. That means He put up with barrenness for nine growing seasons! Nine times he came to that tree and said, "Please, show me some fruit. Show me anything, anything but leaves."

If you are a backslider, then God is saying to you, "Please, I've come to you nine times. I've come in the spring, summer, and fall. I've given you tracts. I've given you gospel messages. I've given you witnesses door to door. I've given you friends who love Me. I've given you *everything*. When am I going to see you turn toward Me? When are you going to respond and choose life?" (Are you paying attention? Are you just going through this chapter, or are you allowing this chaper to go through you?)

By the way: *God is the timekeeper*, not you. He is keeping tabs on all the time you spend not responding to His message. He made a note of the effort you put forth to quench the gentle wooing of His Holy Spirit. He visited your field and saw the barrenness of your tree— despite plea upon earnest plea through gospel tracts, preaching, and Christian witnessing. He marked down the weeks, the months, and the years of your fruitlessness. Despite the tender care of God the Father, you are still not responding, and you are still fruitless.

God has brought you through bitter winters in your life. Like the fruit farmers in the South who tend blazing fires around the clock when a cold snap threatens the sensitive buds in their fruit orchards, God cared for you. Night after night, year after year, God was the only one keeping the frigid winds of adversity from destroying your life. He was there keeping you alive and bringing you through it. But when harvest time rolled around, once again He came to your tree hoping for fruit and walked away in disappointment—nothing was there.

Have you forgotten the times He saved you from locusts, from the destructive parasites seeking to sap your strength through financial failure, depression, or sickness? When you prayed for help, He brought you through by His grace and mercy, friend. But once you got to the end of it and people asked you, "How is everything with your business?" You told them, "Well, I got through it all right. Yeah, my wife and I are doing good now." You didn't say a word about God. Not a word about Jesus. Not a word about the people who prayed for you through lonely nights. Not a word about the time you sought the Bible for an answer and the Lord spoke to you and said, "Trust in the Lord with all thine heart; and lean not unto thine own understanding. In all thy

ways acknowledge Him, and He shall direct thy paths"
(Prov. 3:5-6). No sign of fruit here.

Fruit. God is looking for fruit. He is looking for a little praise, a little thanksgiving, a little opening of your
mouth and giving Him praise publicly, a little talking
about Jesus to your friends. He's looking for fruit.

Number 3: Every tree that does not bear fruit will be cut down and thrown into the fire.

I don't apologize for this Scripture, friend. I cannot
remove it from God's Word. Even if I tried to, other
Scriptures would jump out and scream at me! For in-
stance, Matthew 7:19 says, "Every tree that bringeth not
forth good fruit is hewn down, and cast into the fire."
Then in Matthew 3:10, it says, "And now also the axe is
laid unto the root of the trees: therefore every tree which
bringeth not forth good fruit is hewn down, and cast
into the fire." Matthew Henry was just as blunt:

> "The doom, oh, the doom of barren trees. They
> shall be hewn down and cast into the fire. God will
> deal with them as men used to deal with dried trees
> that cumber the ground. He will mark them by
> some signal tokens of His displeasure. He will cut
> them down to death and cast them into the fires of
> hell, a fire blown with the billows of God's wrath
> and fed with the wood of barren trees."[1]

That is a graphic picture of the end of life, friend.
Solomon said, "To every thing there is a season, and a
time to every purpose under the heaven: a time to be
born, and a time to die; a time to plant, and a time to
pluck up that which is planted" (Eccles. 3:1-2). Why
would God cut you down? I want to tell you why, friend.
According to the Scripture, *you're taking up space.*

I am an evangelist. I have preached throughout America, working in the streets and holding open meetings in city parks. Many of the thousands of shipwrecked people I've met on the streets *were shipwrecked by so-called believers who were fruitless!* The hypocrisy of their fruitless lives drove the hurting away from holding any hope in God. After all, what had He done for those hypocrites? They were fruitless. They were cumbersome, they were using up the soil of God, and they were taking up space. According to this Scripture, friend, the owner of the vineyard has had about all He can take of that kind of tree. He's tired of you taking up valuable space and producing only leaves.

Look at the condition of the church today. Look at who is in our pews. Church pews are filled with trees that are merely full of leaves, friend. God is demanding fruit in this final year. I'm telling you right now, friend, God will cut you down. "I don't believe that, you say." Read the Word. You are shutting out valuable sunlight that another hungrier sapling needs to grow.

Consider the fig tree in Israel that is still full of foliage, blocking out rays of the sun from people who sit beneath it. I see that in Christendom today. Our churches of full of religious old foggies who are just sitting around basking in the sun. Their foliage of leaves is so dense that they are just too fat to move around. If somebody manages to gets saved and wants to get a little sunlight, will you tell them, "Oh no! My, you are too young. You can just sit under my foliage. You'll be just fine"? What happens then, friend? If those young believers do sit underneath you, they will die because there is no fruit in you. You've routed all your energy toward making man-pleasing leaves instead of bearing God-pleasing fruit.

Fertile soil is one of the most precious resources on earth. That is why fruit farmers and vineyard owners keep such a close track of productivity. Whenever they see an older, more established tree reduce its fruit yield, out it comes! They will promptly plant a young sapling in its place so the valuable soil can be used to best effect. God knows exactly what you have produced each year since you were planted. Are you like some big fat fig tree that sees a young sapling planted next to you? When you see that young life in Christ begin to produce a rich crop of fruit, do you draw closer to them hoping to "get what they got" without producing the fruit they produce? Do you start to suck up some of those nutrients while avoiding any kind of commitment? Do you say, "Well, we don't need to be here this long. That was good preaching, Pastor, but come on now. It's time for lunch. I'm just sucking up the nutrients. I'll just suck up everything you say and go on my own way"? Meanwhile, that little tree next to you is absorbing every bit of nourishing truth he can, saying, "Pastor, can you preach till two or three o'clock this afternoon, man? I'm here. Look at me. I'm growing! Look at this—there's a fig!"

Thousands of church pastors come to this revival every week totally worn out, beat up, and dried up because someone sapped all the nutrients in their ministry. They have to tend a vineyard filled with fat, fruitless fig trees that constantly chant, "Feed me. Feed me." Meanwhile, he is begging them, "Produce fruit. Fruit. Yield a harvest before it is too late!" Nevertheless, they are sucking up all the nutrients and complaining, "You need to work harder, Pastor. Work harder! We want more."

How many ministers have been moved out of the way over the years? Kathryn Kuhlman used to say, "I'm only doing the job that a man was supposed to do." Do you know what God did? Somewhere there is a man or men whom God cut off at the base. Somewhere out in God's vineyard there is a nub or a stump, a silent testimony to the heritage of the fruitless fig tree.

Kathryn Kuhlman asked God why He chose her, a woman, to do such a mighty ministry work in an era dominated by men. He told her He had asked seven men before her, but not one would accept the call. Somewhere out there, friend, there is just a row of stumps left marking the day seven different men refused the call of God. Seven times God went to chosen men and said, "I told you to heal the masses. I've anointed you with the Holy Ghost. I've anointed you to heal the sick and the lame. I gave you the authority to touch blind eyes and see them open in My name. Get out there and go to work. Bear fruit for My glory. Please."

God finally turned to a self-conscious but obedient woman named Kathryn and said, "Well, will you do it?" "Yes, sir. I'll do anything for You." Then turning to His last fruitless tree of choice, He said, "Then get out of My way, buddy. You're coming down. I have found another who will do My bidding." Someone went down, friend. I believe that with all of my heart. Throughout her ministry to the sick and the hurting, Kathryn Kuhlman would say over and over again, "I'm only doing the work that others were called to do. It is just that they would not do it."

I believe that if Pastor John Kilpatrick or I stepped out of this pulpit and turned our back on the revival, we would be out of God's will in a heartbeat. I also believe that we would soon hear the sound of the Vinedresser's cart approaching us in the field, and we would soon feel the bite of the Vinedresser's ax. We would hear it coming, friend, because we stepped out of God's will.

God would say to us, "I was the one causing that fruit to grow. I was doing it all. Why on earth did you step out of that revival? Why did you step aside? Now I have to raise up somebody else. It is over for you now. Don't you understand that I had a call on your life? But you stepped out." Suddenly, we would find ourselves over there on the sidelines, bearing only leaves. Friend, God demands fruit from His trees—no matter what they call themselves, no matter what they have done in the past or how well-known they are among men.

You may be in shock right now, but this is a wake-up call. Many of us would have been cut down long ago if it wasn't for Jesus the Mediator. Jonathan Edwards used to say that God's wrath builds up like water behind a dam that is about to burst forth, rising higher and higher. I can see Jesus saying, "Father, give Me another day with him. Give Me just one more day to bring him around." "But My Son, he is a rebel. He will never turn." "Give Me another day with him, Father." Then I see Jesus putting His hand up against that dam and holding back the wrath of God.

How many times has God's pruning ax been placed back in the cart spiritually speaking after the Holy Spirit had already lifted it and stepped into position at the base of your tree? He was walking over to the base of your tree and setting His stance when Jesus stepped in front of Him and said, "The Father just gave Me a few more weeks with this one. I'm going to try one more thing— I'll head him toward the Brownsville Revival to get saved. Put the ax back for a few more days so I can have a little bit more time."

That is called mercy, friend. Jesus Christ is all that stands between Heaven and hell, friend. He said, "Father, Steve Hill is going to get saved. I know he's a rebel, and I know he's on drugs. I even know about his criminal record. The courts of men say he's a menace to society, but give Me just one more week. It's only October 21, 1975. I know he's going to get saved on October 28. Give Me a little more time." That was when the Father said, "Okay. I'll stay My wrath. You've got a week."

Oh, when the Savior steps in, spare Him the humiliation of writing you off forever, friend. Read the Word for yourself just one more time:

> *Behold, these three years I come seeking fruit on this fig tree, and find none: cut it down; why cumbereth it* [why does it use up] *the ground? And he answering said unto him, Lord, let it alone this year also, till I shall dig about it, and dung it: and if it bear fruit, well; and if not, then after that thou shalt cut it down* (Luke 13:7b-9).

Here's the problem, friend. He stepped in and did an intense work in your life. He has done everything He can. He has watered and fertilized you. He has cared for you. He turned the soil around the base of your tree for years. He poked holes way down into the earth and dropped in fertilizer. He cared for your life, but you kept rebelling. Leaves.

He's been doing a lot for you. Isn't it time for you to do something? What day is today? Think of this date on the calendar and remember that no one fully understands God's timetable. You may feel like you have tomorrow, but tomorrow is a word found only in a fool's calendar. How do you know *today* is not going to be your last chance? How do you know tomorrow will come for you?

Where is the ax that is going to come chop you down? Is it still in the shed, or can you hear the rustling of some oxen and an ox cart? Is there an ax laid across the seat of the ox cart? Can you hear the wheels running across the ground, coming closer and closer toward you? As you crash to the ground under the weight of your useless leaves, can you hear the fruit dropping from other trees in the vineyard? You've been bearing and bearing for years—yet there is nothing. What is it like? Is that ax pulling up to your life right now? Maybe it is in the hands of the Keeper of the vineyard. If you don't believe in the judgment of God, then you don't believe the Bible.

Jesus said, "As it was in the days of Noah..." (Lk. 17:26). Friend, there were thousands upon thousands of proud people who did not believe in the judgment of God in Noah's day too, and they bobbed like corks in the water until they finally died. I've heard people say, "I don't believe God would do anything like that." That is a damnable heresy that is spreading across this nation. Yes, God is love, but the Bible also teaches that our loving Savior will one day be a severe Judge. Jesus Christ is calling this nation to repentance, and He is also checking your tree looking for fruit!

Is your life full of leaves? Do you need to save yourself from the blade of the ax of God? Yes, He loves you, but He also demands fruit. The first fruit He requires is true repentance, and you can produce true fruit right now. Don't delay.

One man came up to me and said, "God will never do anything like that." I said, "What book do you read? Who killed Ananias and Sapphira? The Holy Ghost killed them, friend. Look through church history, friend."

If you know you are away from God or that you haven't produced any fruit in years, then you need to do something about it *now*. The only thing that matters to me is that you become destined for Heaven, that you get right with God, and that when you lay down this book you do it in right relationship with the Lord. I want you to pass this book along to another person with fruit just hanging from your tree. That can happen instantaneously. Begin with the rich fruit of repentance. The Bible says that all Heaven rejoices when one person repents and turns to God (see Lk. 15:7).

Do not hesitate. If there is sin in your life, then you need to get right with God. His Son was crucified for you 2,000 years ago. It's time for you to do something for Him. Come to Him on your knees. It is good for you to be on your face before God. Friend, check the tree. Look up at your branches. Do you see repentance or holiness there? What is hanging from your tree? I pray that you do not hear the sound of an approaching ox cart, or the swish of the Vinekeeper's blade sweeping through the air toward the base of your tree. The Scripture says, "Let it alone this year also...and if it bear fruit, well; and if not, then after that *thou shalt cut it down*" (Lk. 13:8b-9). Unlike our false understandings about God's mercy, this Scripture shows there is an end to it.

There are a lot of Scripture verses that stop suddenly just like that. If people were given an opportunity to get saved and they didn't, God often cut them off right there, and Christ moved on. The Bible moves on. The Word moves on. The Church moves on. And right now, we're moving on. You need to act now if there is no fruit in your life. Check that tree and fall to your knees if necessary. There is an urgency in the air. Something is up. If you are tired of producing worthless leaves, if you are convicted by the Holy Spirit because you have failed to produce fruit for the Master year after year, I want you to pray this prayer out loud right now:

Dear Jesus, I'm thankful that I can talk to You. Thank You for sparing my life. Thank You for giving me hope and for speaking to me. Holy Spirit, I thank You for not leaving me alone. I ask You, sweet Jesus, to forgive me. I have sinned and I have hurt You and others besides. I repent of my sins. Wash my sins away; wash me clean and make me new. I want to bear much fruit for You. I want You to be pleased with me. I ask You to be my Savior, my Lord, and my very best friend. From this moment, I am Yours and You are mine. You can count on me. I will bear much fruit. In Your precious name I pray, Lord Jesus. Amen.

Endnote

Matthew Henry, *An Exposition of the Old and New Testament*, vol. 5 (Fleming H. Revell).

Chapter 4

Three Strikes and You're Out

One of my mentors was Leonard Ravenhill. Before he died at the age of 87, I was privileged to spend hours with him on a weekly basis over a period of three years. He was as on fire for God in his 80's as he was when he was a teenager. It was common for him to go after God six hours or more a day, in prayer. Dr. Michael Brown, President of Brownsville Revival School of Ministry, was also being discipled by Brother Ravenhill during this same period. Although Mike was living in Maryland at the time, and traveling extensively, we became friends through this mentoring. Often, when we would speak with Brother Leonard, he would have a new, fresh word from the Lord that would rock us to our toes. He used to say, "Stevie, sit down. The Lord spoke to me at three o'clock in the morning. By the way, what were you doing at three o'clock?" He was direct and to the point, and he had high expectations of serious young men in the ministry. He would say, "The Lord woke me up and told me to tell you this, Stevie. It's in the Book of Second Timothy…Listen, this is for you…." Every time this happened, I remember thinking in amazement, *God, this man is in his 80's.*

The influence of men and women who dare to stand for God without compromise can extend far beyond their lifetimes. I will never forget the day I went to the graveyard where Leonard Ravenhill was buried. Right next to his tombstone is Keith Green's. Keith was buried holding his two children in his arms. His epitaph reads: "Gone to be with Jesus." Like Leonard's it didn't say, "Rest in Peace," or "He was a lovely man," even though they both were. Fortunately, the epitaphs of both men are as unique as they were.

Leonard's stone does not read, "He fought the good fight," although that is a great Scripture and a true statement of his life. As I approached the grave site, I was thinking of Leonard and how he would point his authoritative finger in my face when driving home a point that he knew I needed to accept. I remember walking solemnly up to the grave; I had lost a friend, and I was still deep in thought with my eyes focused on the path before me. I didn't have any flowers; I brought only my thoughts and memories. My eyes naturally landed on the foot of the relatively new grave, and I worked my way up to the tombstone. As I reached the epitaph, it was suddenly as if that same finger was right in my face as I read one of Leonard's trademark questions, which he had asked to be inscribed on his stone:

Are the things you're living for worth Christ dying for?

He had done it again! Even after his death, he had caught me off guard. I thought to myself, *Leonard, don't you ever stop? Rest in peace, my brother.*

Leonard Ravenhill was an overcomer. He didn't believe in soft Christianity. His philosophy was that if Christ gave His all for us, the least we can do is give our all for Him. We have an entire generation of Christians who need to learn that simple truth all over again. We have more knowledge about the Word than any other generation before us, but we may well be the most defeated, selfish, and spineless generation to ever name the name of Christ. God is out to change that by lighting a fire under our carefully padded pews. He wants a spotless Church filled with overcomers.

And I heard a loud voice saying in heaven, Now is come salvation, and strength, and the kingdom of our God, and the power of His Christ: for the accuser of our brethren is cast down, which accused them before our God day and night. And they overcame him by the blood of the Lamb, and by the word of their testimony; and they loved not their lives unto the death (Revelation 12:10-11).

As I was reading this Scripture, I looked closer at the word *they* where the passage says, "And *they* overcame him..." (Rev. 12:11a). Do you know what that means? It means that *you* can be a *they*. You can be one of the overcomers described in the Book of Revelation if you are willing to take the steps outlined by John in that passage. You can insert your own name in that verse: "Sheila overcame him. Bruce overcame him. Bob overcame him, and so did Bill and Marsha." You can be one of them, friend.

Overcomers aren't born, they are reborn in Christ. In other words, you have to be saved before you can be an overcomer. The Bible says, "For whosoever shall call upon the name of the Lord shall be saved" (Rom. 10:13). Do you know who that is? That is everybody, anybody, everyone, him, her, them, they, those. It's me. It's you. It's us, ourselves, themselves, you'ns. Ha! Ya'all. It's amazing to see how God breaks down the language barriers in this revival, friend. People come from all over, and they share their testimonies with us.

You'ns; y'all, us'ns, we, we'ns; you's guys, you guys, all,
each person, that individual, all the people, kids, adoles-
cents, old folks, young folks,
city slickers, farm boys, home boys, hamburger flippers, ice
cream dippers, teeter totter riders, fearless skydivers, short or-
der cooks and collectors of books,
smart people that teach, and mooches that leach, Michigan-
ders from Kalamazoo, and citizens of Timbuktu,
butchers and bakers, and candlestick makers,
anybody can be saved. Whosoever, that is you! There is
hope. Hallelujah!

I am preaching from a passage in the Book of Revelation that begins with the word *they*. Who is that?

You can be big, small, tall, short,
full-headed, grey-headed, bald headed, headed for bald
headed, big boned, medium boned, small boned, blond hair,
black hair, red hair, green hair, gross hair,
red, yellow, black, or white. You are precious in His sight.
You can be sort of bad, sort of real bad, really bad, baddest
of bad, or king of bad.
You can live uptown, downtown, out of town, suburbs, big
house, small house, no house, jailhouse, little house on the
prairie, penthouse in Pittsburgh, Days Inn in downtown
Dayton.
You can be from West Africa, Australia, Ireland, Japan,
Germany, Saudi Arabia, Mexico,
South Korea, the Virgin Islands, Canada, Scotland, Nor-
way, Italy, or Bobo, Alabama. (And that is a place.)

You can be a Jew from Jerusalem or a Gentile from Jacksonville.
You can play the banjo or be named Joe and play in a band.
You can be so smart that you can say the ABC's backward
or be so backward you never learned the ABC's. You can
hold the Guiness Book of World Records for eating the

most live slugs
or have a collection of the world's most colorful bugs. You
can be visiting this revival like everybody "oughta"
or come walking off the streets from Boston just to get a
drink of "wata."

I am doing my best to cover everybody who will ever read this book. Stay with me; I'm not finished. You say, "Dear Jesus, speak to my heart, change my life." He's trying to, friend. He's trying to *include* you right now. Get included, would you?

You can be patriotic, wearing red, white, and blue and be
sitting by your friend who has a big tattoo.
You can be a shepherd from the hills or a pusher of pills, a
wise man from afar or a soap opera star.
You can be a Methodist from Montana or a Jew from Japan,
be a vegetarian from Virginia or a connoisseur of Spam.
You can come from Texas in a Lexus with spurs in your
heels, or be a fly fisherman from Frankfurt with 15 shiny
reels.
You can make your living churning delicious homemade
butter, or spend every day collecting cans in the city gutter.
You can play a guitar and be an international star, or be a
clown in a circus driving the world's smallest car.
You can be the tidiest person this world has ever known, or
live like a pig with garbage in your home.
You can keep up with the Joneses or be the Jones' house-
keeper or maybe the coolest dude in school with the largest
florescent beeper.
You can smell like Chanel and live like a queen, or make
your abode in an alley wearing tattered Levi jeans.
You can drive a BMW and wear flashy Italian suits or ride
an Appaloosa sporting pointed cowboy boots.
It doesn't make a difference if you're happy or you're blue,

just call upon the Lord, whosoever, that's you!
That's you! Hallelujah! That's me.

Well, I just wanted to lay a firm foundation before moving on to the next point, because it gets tougher from here on. It should be obvious that for someone to be called an overcomer, there had to be some type of battle or obstacle to overcome. The fact is, *we are at war.* Did you realize that? It is the longest war in history. This war didn't stop at the 25-year mark; it has never stopped and it has been going on since the beginning, friend. It is the war with satan, the ongoing battle between good and evil in the earth.

How did the saints in Revelation 12:10 overcome and conquer their adversary? And exactly who is this adversary anyway? He has many names and aliases, including lucifer (shining one), and satan (adversary, accuser). He is also known as the son of the morning, accuser of the brethren, the adversary, the angel from the bottomless pit, beelzebub (the lord of the flies), the god of this world, the old serpent, the murderer, the father of lies, the ruler of darkness, the wicked one, and the prince of the power of the air.

He is old and experienced. He is daring, and he goes after big game. He went after Jesus Christ and each of the apostles, including Peter and Paul. He'll go after you too. He is angry and malicious because he was totally humiliated and defeated when he tried to take over Heaven, and again when Jesus invaded the realm of hell, death, and the grave. Now he is trying to take over the earth. He is watchful and crafty, like a wolf in sheep's clothing. If you are thinking, "Dear God, man, he sounds pretty powerful," let me tell you who he is up against.

Every time I meet a Christian with his head hanging down, I wonder, *Have you met Him? Do you have any idea what the word **Christian** means? Do you have any idea who lives in you?* He happens to be the Almighty, the Alpha and Omega, the Beginning and the End, the Anointed of the Lord, the Head of all things, the great High Priest, the Judge of the living and the dead, the Chief Cornerstone, the Bright and Morning Star, the King of kings and the Lord of lords, and the Creator of the universe. He is El Shaddai, God Almighty. He's the everlasting God. He's the Holy One of Israel. He is eternal God, the living God. I'm telling you, friend, this is what lucifer has been up against from the very beginning. And he knows he is doomed.

Satan the rebel is up against the Lion of the tribe of Judah, the Lily of the Valley, the Rock of Ages, the Lamb of God who takes away the sin of the world. He is Jehovah Jireh, the Bishop of our souls, the Savior of the world, Redeemer, Miracle Worker. He's the Healer of our bodies. He's Immanuel, God with us. He is the Sacrificed Lamb that was slain before the foundation of the world, God's beloved Son in whom He is well pleased, incomparable, invincible, unchangeable, unequaled. He is infinite, eternal, omnipotent, omnipresent, omniscient. He is full of love, truth, mercy, vengeance, and wrath. He is the Alpha and the Omega. Friend, He is the Christ, the Son of the living God. That's who He is. Hallelujah! Jesus. Jesus. Jesus.

The devil and his demons tremble at that name. Jesus Christ will heal your body, save your soul, and set you free. Hallelujah! Let me tell you more about that name, friend. I was saved by that name. The Lutheran vicar who led me to the Lord did not share with me the four spiritual laws (although I thank God for them). He did not share with me "the Roman road to salvation" (and I thank God for those too). That man didn't even explain the cross to me. He just came into my bedroom and said, "Steve, just say the name Jesus."

I had been a druggie for 12 years. I was a thief and a hopeless drug addict. I had been in and out of jails all over the country, and I was so wasted that I felt like my life was over. Many of my friends were dead and gone by the time that man came into my room. He didn't even force me to pray. He just said, "Pray with me." When I said, "I don't know how to pray," he replied, "That's fine. You don't have to pray. Just say the name, *Jesus*."

My friend, satan has never recognized the Assemblies of God. Lucifer has never recognized the Southern Baptist Church, the American Baptists, the Primitive Baptists, or even the United Methodist Church. The different synods of the Presbyterian Church, the Episcopal Church, the Lutheran Church, the Church of the Brethren, the Roman Catholic Church, the Christian Church, and the Church of God denominations have never meant a thing to him. Those are just organizations. There are wonderful Christians in every one of them, but their denominational name tags have no power to rub satan the wrong way or make him shake. However, when you say the name of Jesus, all hell stands at attention! At the name of Jesus, every demon in hell begins to shake in uncontrollable fear.

I want you to understand that you have a bitter enemy, friend. The good news is that the Bible says you can overcome him. Now let me tell you what it *does not* say. The Bible does not say, "and they overcame him by coming to the Brownsville Revival, by being prayed for every night, and by singing with Lindell Cooley at the top of their lungs." These things are great and wonderful, but the Bible does not say they are the key to overcoming the devil. I don't care if you have the latest edition of the "Revised Revival Version" of the Bible (it doesn't exist to my knowledge, so don't ask for it at your local Christian bookstore). The Bible does not say that you will overcome satan by calling him a snot, and it doesn't say he will fall if you simply avoid involving yourself in séances and if you stay away from voodoo dolls and Ouija boards. You cannot overcome satan by faithfully attending the church of your choice any more than you can by cooking your hamburgers on the ground instead of over a stove. You don't overcome the devil by telling the pastor he's the most important person since Billy Graham. The Bible does not say that you overcome the adversary by "turning over a new leaf," by giving a good offering, or by helping local Christmas charities collect toys for tots and jeans for teens. That's not what the Bible says, friend.

The Bible lists three things for overcomers. You could think of them as a spiritual litmus test for your life. You are going to see exactly why you can't stand up under demonic onslaughts. You will know beyond a shadow of a doubt whether or not you are lukewarm or as cold as they come. It is my opinion that if these three things are not found in your life when the Lord comes back, then you will be dragged into hell in a heartbeat. Now you know why I want you to pay close attention to God's Word.

I have to warn you that this might hurt. Sometimes I feel like a surgeon, because I know that sometimes you have to make your patients hurt before they get better.

Any doctor worth his salt is so determined to cure his patients that he or she could care less if they have to scream out in pain every now and then. If the doctor has to break a bone to reset it, then that bone will be broken and reset, because that may be the only way the patient will walk properly in the future. Doctors have to put up with all kinds of crying, complaining, and screaming, but they will do it if it means they can help heal you. And that is what this is all about.

Any good preacher thinks the same way. Pastor, that is the only way to truly serve God and minister to your congregation. That's what I love about Pastor John Kilpatrick—he'll share the truth even if he has us all screaming until the last two minutes of his message. Some may stomp out saying, "Who does that man think he is?!" But 98 out of 100 will say, "Boy, that man must love me. He is willing to risk my anger just to tell me the truth and make me whole."

Satan is at the plate and you are on the pitcher's mound. What are you going to throw satan's way? I know you've been steeped in the "circle the wagons" mentality. I know many think the devil should be the pitcher and they should be facing him with a stick, but God sees things differently. In His Kingdom, the children of the King hold all the power and authority, and the children of darkness are on the losing side. It is time to change your perspective.

Strike Number One

The rule of the game is this: "Three strikes and you're out, devil." According to the Word of God, this is your first pitch: "They overcame him by the Blood of the Lamb" (**Rev. 12:11a**). I'm going to say that again: *They* *overcame him by the Blood of the Lamb.* Are you washed in the Blood of the Lamb?

I've lost count of the times I've preached on the power of the Blood of Jesus in this revival. I'll never get tired of it because it will never ever lose its power. I know the men and women who witnessed the crucifixion of Jesus Christ 2,000 years ago heard and saw a lot of things. But I believe that what burned into their memories most indelibly was the drip, drip, drip of the Savior's precious Blood. They saw it drip from His precious brow. They saw it flow from His wounded hands, down His arms, onto that rugged cross, and into the cursed soil of Golgotha Hill to redeem a fallen race from the curse of sin and death.

The Bible says, "...without shedding of blood is no remission [of sin]" (Heb. 9:22). Without the shedding of Blood, there is no forgiveness. There are multitudes of sincerely religious folks who are trying to work their way to Heaven by selling leaflets or flowers, by going to door-to-door to win people over to their beliefs, and by doing this or that. It's all for naught. God says only the Blood of Christ can save you. Your only hope rests in what God's only Son did on Calvary 2,000 years ago. Our salvation is only found on the cross, in the Blood, through the Lamb of God who took away the sin of the world. Only Jesus can save you, friend. He is the only One.

America is trying everything else to get to Heaven, friend, but it isn't working. There is forgiveness in the Blood of Christ. Every time we sing about the Blood, my heart leaps, because I remember the moment 21 years ago when I was covered in the Blood and was saved. The Blood of Jesus Christ soaked me and washed my sins away. Suddenly I was no longer guilty, but moments before I had been as guilty as guilty can be. I said, "Jesus, wash my sins away. I look to the cross. You shed Your Blood for me. Father, I'm looking to Your Son. He did it for me. He is my forgiveness." I believe Jesus looked toward His Father and said, "It's done. On October 28, 1975, at 11:00 in the morning, Father, Steve Hill was washed in the Blood of the Lamb." I was cleansed, friend, but it was nothing but the Blood.

You will never ever overcome the wicked one if you have not been washed in the Blood of the Lamb. Perhaps you were washed in the Blood of the Lamb 12 or 15 years ago, and you've been taught that it's a one-time event. Now you wonder why you are as cold as ice and dry as toast! The answer is that you have wandered far away from God. Your need for the Blood is not a "one-time thing" friend. Yes, you get saved once, but you need to be cleansed, restored, and renewed daily. You need to plead the Blood every time you face the adversary of your soul! Read the Book of Revelation if you doubt my words!

The reason backsliders are so miserable is they don't understand what's happened. They got saved 12 years ago in a revival meeting or at church, but for some reason "it's not sticking." Friend, Christianity is an ongoing relationship, not a one-time event. You come before the Lord daily and pray, "Wash me in Your Blood, Lord Jesus. Cleanse me anew." It is vital that you understand that before we go on to another point. You need to go back to the very beginning and return to your first love so you can get washed in His Blood.

One man recently told me during a revival service, "I feel so dirty. I feel unclean. I was saved years ago, but I feel dirty." I told him, "You need to be washed in the

Blood of the Lamb, sir." You don't overcome satan by telling him you're a member of Brownsville Assembly of God or First Baptist Church. You don't overcome satan by telling him you come to the revival all the time, or by "shaking under the power" on the floor! You don't overcome satan by "falling under the power." Those things have nothing to do with it. The devil doesn't even recognize that stuff. What he recognizes—and fears—is the Blood. When he sees the Blood of Jesus, he knows it's over. The saints in Revelation 12:11 overcame satan by the Blood of the Lamb.

Strike Number Two

Satan hates to see you throw the Blood of the Lamb in his face. He always swings at dead air when that deadly pitch comes his way. Now what will you do? He's madder than ever. Turn to God's Word and see what signal He is giving you: "And they overcame him by the blood of the Lamb, and *by the word of their testimony...*" (Rev. 12:11).

A testimony is "firsthand authentication of a fact: evidence; an open acknowledgment; a public profession of a religious experience."[1] It is an act of validating the truth or falsehood of something. My definition of a Christian testimony is "an up-to-date account of what Jesus has done and *is* doing in your life." Don't talk to me about what happened to you 18 years ago. I want to see *evidence* that you are saved now. I want to see you on fire right now. That is a testimony.

I love to see the young people in this revival. They are so on fire that you had better get out of their way. Many times I will meet with them in a hallway just before revival services because they want me to pray with them before they go out to witness on the streets of their city! Rather than enjoying the service, they fan out through Pensacola's rougher streets to share the Good News. You don't have to ask them if they know Jesus—their lives are a testimony, a witness, a walking demonstration of what the Lord has done for them. When people curse them, or if they throw beer in their face, spit on them, or slap them, they just look at them and say, "Jesus loves you, man. He's changed my life. I was just like you before I got saved, but He will minister to you. He'll heal you."

During the Christmas season, one of our teenagers waited in line at the mall just so she could sit on Santa's lap! Now listen to the rest of the story before you condemn her. In her mind, it was witnessing time. The girl had a captive audience. Every kid and parent in that line was locked in when she sat on Santa's lap. She knew that good old Santa couldn't get mad, and since there was a little elf or some angelic-looking lady taking pictures of the scene, he had to make it look good. The stage was set so this young lady threw Santa a curve ball by boldly saying with a strong voice, "I have just one question to ask you, Santa: Do you know Jesus Christ as your personal Savior? Are you a Christian?" To make things really interesting, she added with a twinkle in her eye, "Now don't you lie, Santa."

I love it. I wish I could say that Santa broke into tears, rolled off his throne, fell to his knees, and repented. He didn't. But the bottom line is that he was confronted. There was no question about it—that teenager landed in Santa's lap for an eternal purpose. That is a testimony, friend. (That doesn't mean we all need to line up to see Santa next December!) The devil hates that inner witness that tells everyone around you that you are a child of

God. God's Word declares that you can overcome the devil by the word of your testimony.

When I got saved I would walk up to my unsaved friends (most of them came up to me), and look directly into their eyes. I didn't have to say anything. They *asked me*, "What's happened to you?" I'd say, "Jesus Christ has changed my life, man." "You've got to be kidding!" "No man. You wouldn't believe the peace I've got in my heart." "Oh come on, Steve. Let's go get stoned." "I don't do that anymore, man. I'm free. I don't need drugs. I don't need pot. I don't need whiskey. I don't need beer. I don't need smokes. I don't need any of that anymore. I'm a free man."

I have to ask you this question: What is your testimony like? Satan knows your testimony, and he knows whether you really know Jesus, or if you are working from outdated or secondhand knowledge. The demons told the seven sons of Sceva, "And the evil spirit answered and said, Jesus I know, and Paul I know; but who are ye? And the man in whom the evil spirit was leaped on them, and overcame them, and prevailed against them..." (Acts 19:15-16). The problem is that these fakers were doing what a lot of people in the churches are trying to do—live off of another man's revelation. They tried to overcome demons by saying, "We adjure you by Jesus whom Paul preacheth" (Acts 19:13b). It doesn't work that way, friend.

I want my name on that "Hell's Most Wanted" list. I want my name to be spoken across the strategy tables every day in hell. I want the devil and his demons to consider "Brownsville" as a curse word down there. As soon as some imp curses, "Brownsville!" I want lucifer to turn around and say, "Shut up, fool. I told you to never say that. But now that you brought it up...watch out for those guys named...." Is your name and testimony known in hell?

Your testimony is a mighty tool, though fragile. It is easily tarnished and destroyed through sin. Robert Murray McCheyne said, "A holy minister is an awful weapon in the hand of God." That applies to ministers as well as everybody else. A Christian should be a *holy* Christian (or change your name!). I see a lot of "Christians" who will talk of wonderful exploits they do for God, but when holiness comes up, they hang their heads because they know their testimony isn't worth beans! Teenager, you can boldly say to your pals at school that you're a Christian and parade around in a T-shirt that says, "Pray Hard." But when you go home, shut your door, and pull out your sex magazine or surf through the sea of cyberporn on the Internet to entertain sexual daydreams, the word of your testimony has been shot! Lucifer saw what you did behind closed doors. Talk till you are blue in the face to your friends, but lucifer already has your number. *You've lost your power!*

Compromise of any kind will destroy your testimony. That applies to all of the "whosoevers." Lucifer knows about your fantasies ma'am. He watches you buy the fantasy novels when you get the family groceries. Lucifer knows that murder is committed first in the mind before it is ever committed in reality. When you see another man and begin imagining what it would be like to go to bed with him, or be married to him and have his children, you just murdered your spouse in your mind! As a man thinks in his heart, so is he. Ladies, when you read those books and imagine yourselves in those situations, you may as well have gone out and openly committed the sin, because your testimony is shot. You can't have the power to overcome the enemy if you are constantly willingly falling prey to his snares. It's time to repent and get real with God. Live holy, preserve your testimony in Christ, and use it with boldness to overcome the devil.

Strike Number Three

The last strike pitch is the one most of us totally miss. I've heard a lot of preachers preach on this passage of Scripture in Revelation 12, but they never cover the last point. There is more. Two strikes will put the devil in a world of hurt, but it takes three strikes to throw him off the plate!

> *...the accuser of our brethren is cast down, which accused them before our God day and night. And they overcame him by the blood of the Lamb, and by the word of their testimony;* **and they loved not their lives unto the death** (Revelation 12:10-11).

These saints were totally sold out. Too many of us are like Paul's friend, Demas. "For Demas hath forsaken me [Paul], having loved this present world, and is departed..." (2 Tim. 4:10). I can see Demas looking at all the people who had homes and families and cars (or the "latest model" donkey in his day). I think he told himself, *Man, look at all these people have. I don't have anything, Paul.* Is that your weak point? Do you love this present world too much to give your all for Christ?

If you have backslidden, ask yourself, "Why did I backslide? What did I love more than Jesus?" Was it a career? A partner who wasn't on fire for God? A drink? The party life? What caused you to turn away? I'm concerned, friend. If you love the Lord and are zealous for God, it will confound your enemy and confirm your allegiance.

You may be washed in the Blood, and you may have a powerful testimony, but what about point number three? If you love your life too much, you've given the devil yet another chance. Think about it: What do you do with a person like Paul who says, "To die is gain"?

A friend of mine named Mickey was in Chicago when two hoodlums jumped into his car— one pressing a gun to his forehead. They yelled, "Give us your money or we'll kill you!" Mickey grinned real big and said, "Do you mean it?" They said, "Of course we mean it! We'll kill you, man!" Then, much to their astonishment, Mickey said, "Jesus, today is the day!" He turned to the men and said, "SHOOT!" (This is a true story, friend.) His response so shocked the two men that one went berserk and ran out of the car. The thug who remained continued pressing for Mickey's money, but Mickey just said, "You can't have my money. You can kill me if you want to. Whether I live or die, I belong to Jesus!" The remaining guy got saved right then and there! Mickey loved not his life unto death. In fact, he got so excited at the prospect of meeting Jesus face to face, that he had an eternal effect on those around him.

This kind of total devotion to Christ is considered part of the normal Christian life in the Bible and throughout the history of the church. According to church history and various verbal traditions handed down from generation to generation, the 11 ruffians who followed Jesus all the way to the cross willingly paid a price for their devotion. We know what happened with Judas, but what happened to the rest of them? Andrew died in Greece after being crucified on an X-shaped cross. He told his executioners he felt unworthy to die on the same type of cross as His Lord. Bartholomew preached the gospel in India and died a martyr's death after being filleted alive with knives. James the elder was the first disciple to be martyred. He died at the hands of Herod Agrippa. James the lessor was crucified in Egypt and his body was sawn in pieces. John the Revelator was spared by divine intervention after an attempt was made to poison his chalice of water or wine. He alone of the original 12 apostles of the Lamb is known to have died of natural causes. Jude was shot with arrows on Mount Ararat, and according to church history, Matthew laid down his life for Jesus as a missionary and disappeared during his labors. Peter died a martyr's death after being crucified upside down. He also felt he was not worthy to die as his Lord had died. Philip died by hanging, but he asked that his body not be wrapped in fine linen. He felt he was not worthy to have his body treated in the same manner as the body of Jesus. Tradition says Simon the Zealot died on the mission field as a martyr, and Thomas, who was commissioned to build a palace for the king of India, was killed with a spear as a martyr for the sake of the gospel.

Stay with me; this part hurts. They loved not their lives unto death. The love of this life did not stand in competition with their loyalty to Christ. Backslider, why did you backslide? What did you fall in love with more than Jesus? What comforts of this earth do you allow to compete with your allegiance to Jesus? I'm concerned for you, friend. We are talking about overcomers—those whose own lives are given over to stronger affections—with courage and zeal for the cause of Christ.

This type of devotion wasn't limited to the original disciples. In my library I have a three-volume set of *Foxes' Book of Martyrs*, from the year 1684. Three volumes! Each of these books is about 17 inches tall by 12 inches wide with a thick leather cover. At three to four inches thick, they go about 850 pages each. Each page is filled top to bottom with about four columns of print, smaller than what you are reading right now. Think about that for a minute—about 2,550 pages of actual, graphic accounts of families martyred for not renouncing their faith in Christ. (Today's edition of *Foxes' Book of Martyrs*, waters down their cries into a five-by-seven-inch volume about one inch thick. We don't want the whole story today, or perhaps we don't have time for it. Put a pretty cover on it, take out the pictures, and make it nice.) You can open up to any of those huge pages and cringe as you find testimony after testimony of Blood-washed Christians, who loved not their lives unto often horrifying deaths.

Families were burned at the stake. Parents were made to watch their children be cut to pieces, and with each limb or finger Daddy was told, "Deny Christ, then you and your family can live." I believe all Heaven would stand in reverent attention as Mom and Dad and the children bravely replied, "No. We love the Lord more than this life!"

If you were to walk into my study, you would see a huge, antique picture on the wall that dates from the 1800's. It depicts a place like an old Roman arena where people were being martyred for their faith in Christ. I walk in there every day and sometimes stare at the picture for a few moments before preparing my message. I have prayed, "Jesus, at the marriage supper of the Lamb, I want to be able to talk to those little girls who are being ripped apart by lions, and to those men who are there being eaten alive for Your name's sake." You see, friend, I want to be able to look them in the eye, and have them look at me. I want them to be able to say, "Well done, Steve." I'm going to say, "Man, you guys inspired me." They will probably say, "Oh, we didn't do anything but live for Jesus; you did that." "No, you don't understand the society I came from. We were a bunch of wimps. If someone so much as cursed us, many would bow their heads in shame and walk away. If following the One who died for us meant giving up the comforts of this world, we debated about whether we could give up wine with dinner to be with Him forever...."

Three strikes and you're out, not two strikes and a "walk." If you start throwing your third pitch with a weak arm—weak conviction, weak commitment—you'll let the devil "walk" all over your life. I'm talking about you overcoming satan by the Blood of the Lamb, the word of your testimony, and by a firm determination to love not your life unto death. That means you will say to every adversary and persecutor who wants to deprive you of life or liberty for the sake of your faith: "Do whatever you want to do to me, but I love Jesus Christ with all of my heart, soul, and strength. I will not deny Him though it cost me my life."

Not long ago I received a phone call from a man who had a vision about me. He said, "Steve, you've been marked as a martyr. People want to do away with your life." Now, whenever I hear something like that, it does not bother me. I'm not perfect, and I don't consider myself better than anyone else, but Jesus has done such a work in my life that I have been changed. I just said, "Jesus, could it be possible, Lord, for me to die in Your work? Would it be conceivable to shed my blood for Your name? You shed Your Blood for me. Would it be possible for me to die in the midst of a great revival? I would count it an honor, Lord, if You permit that to happen." Frankly, with that kind of attitude, I can see the Lord dispatching angels and saying, "Nothing is going to happen to you, boy."

It's like my friend Mickey whom I told you about earlier. His first thought was not for his possessions or his life. It was for his Savior, so that is what came out of his mouth first! Those of you who fear for your own life— you talk about your life. Your conversation is filled with your possessions and your positions. You need to act like a man, or woman, of God and be strong. You need to stand up and say, "I'm a Christian. I love the Lord with all my heart, soul, and strength. Though none go with me, still I will follow!"

How about you? Are you washed in the Blood of the Lamb? Are your sins, though scarlet, made white as snow in His cleansing? Will your testimony stand the heat of adversity, or will it crumble in the face of the enemy? Are you ashamed of the Lord? Are the things of this world still luring you to two-time Jesus? Friend, if you can't strike out the devil on all three areas, lucifer has your number! He's saying, "This man will never make it in the day of battle. This woman will never make it when the heat is on. They can handle revival. They love to sing. She loves it when things are wonderful and thrilling, clapping, jumping, and waving her baton. But they will never be overcomers."

People are still being martyred for their faith today, you know. It was reported that 100,000 people were martyred for the cause of Christ last year alone. Two ladies in Cambodia were mowed down with machine guns because they were teaching health classes, along with the gospel of Jesus Christ. A minister in Colombia was murdered by a drug cartel because drug addicts were being saved. How are you going to stand with them on Judgment Day when you can't even hold your head up now, when you deny His Lordship even in the face of some minor persecution? There is hope, friend. I want you to pray this prayer with me out loud, right now:

Dear Jesus, thank You for speaking to me. I need Your forgiveness because I have sinned. I have hurt You and others as well. I repent of my sins. Please forgive me, Jesus, and wash my sins away. Cleanse me and make me new by the Blood of the Lamb. Lord Jesus, I want to be an overcomer by the Blood of the Lamb, by the word of my testimony, and by loving my life not unto death. I want to live for You, Jesus. If necessary, I will die for You. I am willing to do anything for You. I ask You to be my Savior, my Lord, and my very best friend. From this moment on, I am Yours and You are mine. I pray this in Your precious name. Amen.

Chapter 5

The Fellowship of the Uncommitted

There was a man born in England during Queen Elizabeth's reign in the 1500's who became a minister of the gospel. He and his wife lived godly lives and were obedient to the Lord. Their son later settled in the American colonies in what is now Hartford, Connecticut, where he became an honorable businessman. Why? His mother and father were Christians. He followed in their stead, and his son also became a God-fearing businessman who was honored among his peers. This businessman also had a son and he became a minister. He won such honor in his ministerial studies that Harvard University conferred two degrees on him on the same day, one in the morning and one in the afternoon.

This learned man had a son who became a minister as well. (I want you to follow this chain of grace.) This minister had a son who also chose to enter the ministry. This young man named Jonathan Edwards was to become one of the most effective and influential evangelists in the history of North America. By the beginning of the 1900's, this family that had sprung from one man and woman who decided to live uncompromised lives for

God—people who decided not to drink, curse, or frequent barrooms; people who were committed to live upright and holy before God and to pass that heritage on to their children—had produced one of the most enviable heritages in this nation.

By the turn of this century, the 1,394 descendants of this man identified and verified by researchers included 295 college graduates, 13 college presidents, 65 college professors, 60 physicians, 108 preachers of the gospel, 101 lawyers, 30 judges, 1 Vice President of the United States, 75 Army and Navy officers, 60 prominent authors, and 16 railroad and shipping presidents. Just as amazing is the fact that in the entire record of the Edwards' family, not one person had ever gone to jail for a crime! Godliness sounds like a sure prescription for what ails this nation! Think about it, friend. This is the fruit of commitment.

On the other hand, there is a large group of people who are in serious danger today. This group has been around since the beginning of time, and they have been instrumental in leading millions of people away from truth of the cross and the crucifixion. This group is often very opinionated. When its members are confronted with the facts, they often run away or lash out like cornered animals. Members of this group were nailed to the wall by Jesus, Paul the apostle, John the revelator, and many of the other writers of Holy Scripture. Membership in this group often comes in subtle ways, and many adherents have slipped in gradually. But before long they found themselves fully indoctrinated and totally unaware that so much evil had affected them so quickly. I speak of the "Fellowship of the Uncommitted."

Since it is no accident that you are reading this book, it is likely that you have entered an appointment with destiny. You are destined to get on fire for God as never before as you read God's Word in this message. One Baptist pastor from Nashville, Tennessee, called my office and told me between his sobs, "Brother Steve, I am sick and tired of religion. I'm sick and tired of church. I'm sick and tired of no power. I'm sick and tired of no deliverances. I'm sick and tired of people not getting saved. I'm sick and tired of griping Christians. I'm sick and tired of all of it. I want a difference in my life. I want a change in my life. I want the power to come down in my church!"

Then he said, "Somebody told me about your revival there in Brownsville. Would you tell me—is it real?" Don't ever ask me that question. We've been here since Father's Day of 1995, and we've seen more than 100,000 people stream to the altar to be saved or get right with God. I was able to tell this man who was so sick and tired of "ho-hum" Christianity, "Brother, it's *real!*" The lost are saved, the sick are healed, and the fallen are restored through the death, burial, and resurrection of Jesus Christ. God's glory has fallen on this place. But it didn't come about through the labors of the fellowship of the uncommitted.

And it came to pass, that, as they went in the way, a certain man said unto Him, Lord, I will follow Thee whithersoever Thou goest. And Jesus said unto him, Foxes have holes, and birds of the air have nests; but the Son of man hath not where to lay His head. And He said unto another, Follow Me. But he said, Lord, suffer me first to go and bury my father. Jesus said unto him, Let the dead bury their dead: but go thou and preach

*the kingdom of God. And another also said, Lord, I will
follow Thee; but let me first go bid them farewell, which
are at home at my house. And Jesus said unto him, **No
man, having put his hand to the plough, and looking
back, is fit for the kingdom of God*** (Luke 9:57-62).

Stay with me. I'm talking about the fellowship of the
uncommitted.

*And, behold, one came and said unto Him, Good Mas-
ter, what good thing shall I do, that I may have eternal
life? And He said unto him, Why callest thou Me good?
there is none good but one, that is, God: but if thou wilt
enter into life, keep the commandments. He saith unto
Him, Which? Jesus said, Thou shalt do no murder,
Thou shalt not commit adultery, Thou shalt not steal,
Thou shalt not bear false witness, Honour thy father
and thy mother: and, Thou shalt love thy neighbour as
thyself. The young man saith unto Him, All these
things have I kept from my youth up: what lack I yet? Jesus said unto him, If thou wilt be perfect, go and sell
that thou hast, and give to the poor, and thou shalt
have treasure in heaven: and come and follow Me. But
when the young man heard that saying, he went away
sorrowful: for he had great possessions* (Matthew
19:16-22).

There are pastors across this nation who are afraid to
call sinners to repentance in their churches because they
are afraid they will offend their tithers and church deacons. In contrast, Jesus went out of His way to "cull the
herd." He didn't ask for commitment; He demanded it.

The apostle James said, "A double-minded man is unstable in all his ways" (Jas. 1:8). We like to quietly substitute the word *some* for *all* in that verse. That way it hurts
a little less when we have to admit that we are double

minded. The problem is that James said a double minded man is unstable in *all* of his ways *because it is true.*

The Book of Joshua contains a prime example of a double minded man and the consequences of his sin. Nearly every preacher in the world has preached on the fall of Jericho, but what about the sin at Jericho that led to disaster at the battle of Ai? This is a journal of the fellowship of the uncommitted.

> *And the city* [Jericho] *shall be accursed, even it, and all that are therein, to the Lord: only Rahab the harlot shall live, she and all that are with her in the house, because she hid the messengers that we sent. And ye, in any wise keep yourselves from the accursed thing, lest ye make yourselves accursed, when ye take of the accursed thing, and make the camp of Israel a curse, and trouble it. But all the silver, and gold, and vessels of brass and iron, are consecrated unto the Lord: they shall come into the treasury of the Lord* (Joshua 6:17-19).

What do you think the Lord meant? This is what He meant: "All the silver, and gold, and vessels of brass and iron, are consecrated unto the Lord; they shall come into the treasury of the Lord." No embellishment is needed. God is saying, "It's Mine. None of it is for you." Somebody didn't get the message:

> *But the children of Israel committed a trespass in the accursed thing: for **Achan, the son of Carmi, the son of Zabdi, the son of Zerah, of the tribe of Judah, took of the accursed thing: and the anger of the Lord was kindled against the children of Israel.** And Joshua sent men from Jericho to Ai, which is beside Bethaven, on the east side of Bethel, and spake unto them, saying, Go up and view the country. And the men went up and viewed Ai. And they returned to Joshua, and said unto*

him, Let not all the people go up; but let about two or three thousand men go up and smite Ai; and make not all the people to labour thither; for they are but few. So there went up thither of the people about three thousand men: and they fled before the men of Ai. And the men of Ai smote of them about thirty and six men: for they chased them from before the gate even unto Shebarim, and smote them in the going down: wherefore the hearts of the people melted, and became as water (Joshua 7:1-5).

Something had obviously gone wrong. Israel had just whipped a far more dangerous enemy without losing one man. Now 36 men were dead after mighty Israel was defeated by a small force from a tiny city. Joshua was beside himself.

*And Joshua rent his clothes, and fell to the earth upon his face before the ark of the Lord until the eventide, he and the elders of Israel, and put dust upon their heads. And Joshua said...would to God we had been content, and dwelt on the other side Jordan! ... **And the Lord said unto Joshua, Get thee up; wherefore liest thou thus upon thy face? Israel hath sinned,** and they have also transgressed My covenant which I commanded them: for they have even taken of the accursed thing... neither will I be with you any more, except ye **destroy the accursed from among you*** (Joshua 7:6-7,10-12).

Welcome to the fellowship of the uncommitted. Now, I'm going to say something profound: *To be **uncommitted** is to be the opposite of committed.* I told you it was deep. To be committed is to be obligated to, to be sold out, to be actively involved, to be dedicated. The uncommitted person is unenthusiastic, half-hearted, indifferent, and uninterested. He is cool, lukewarm, undecided, hesitant, unresolved. People like this drive me up the wall. They are always passive, apathetic, lackadaisical, uncertain, undetermined, unsettled, up in the air, ambivalent, "iffy," and unfaithful. Proverbs warns about these kind of people, "Confidence in an unfaithful man in time of trouble is like a broken tooth, and a foot out of joint" (Prov. 25:19). What is that look on your face? Are you in pain?

If you are in the Armed Forces and you are uncommitted to the service, you will be discharged. If you are a student and are uncommitted to your studies, you will flunk out. Married person, if you are uncommitted to your mate, you are headed for a divorce. If you're a stockbroker who is uncommitted to your client, you will go broke. If you are a doctor and are uncommitted to your patients, they'll look for a physician who cares. If you are a lawyer and are uncommitted to the law, you will be disbarred. If you are a football player and are uncommitted to the team, you will be cut. If you are a waiter and you're uncommitted to your table, you will be tipless. If you are a Christian and you are uncommitted to Christ, you are heading for serious judgment. There are three important facts you need to know about the fellowship of the uncommitted.

Number 1: The uncommitted are modern-day idol worshipers.

Don't believe the lie that idols are only found somewhere in the lands of the Buddhists or somewhere across the Pacific. No, friend, there are idol worshipers all across America and in every church! *An idol is anything that sets itself up in the place of Christ.* Anything that steals your affection for Christ or cools your love for Him is *idolatry*. Is it possible that there are idols in your life—like your golf game, and your hunting and fishing trips? You are actually worshiping the bass pro fishing shop and bowing down to it if you allow it to displace any part of your devotion for Christ. Actions speak louder than words. Friend, if you invested that kind of time and energy in your walk with Christ, you would shake the world!

I collect old Christian books as a hobby, and I love to read. But that can be an idol too. You have to be careful of anything that takes the place of Christ. Even a book that talks about Christ can be an idol if it becomes a substitute for going after Christ Himself. Would you rather read a book about prayer than actually pray? Beware of the idol. Would you rather read about revival than have revival? Your idol could be a boyfriend, a girlfriend, real estate holdings, your job, money, love for power, your craving for attention, politics, or an extreme love for your family. (Most of the people who say they can't go to a revival because of "family time" have to admit that "family time" in their home consists of planting themselves in front of the television set and turning it on. Is that quality family time? If that's all you do with your kids, it's idol worship.) Friend, your family needs to see you go after God like He is the source of your life and your chief joy. Then you will enjoy true quality time together for a lifetime and eternity, with Christ at the center of your existence.

Those who belong to the fellowship of the uncommitted are modern-day idol worshipers. Look at the rich young ruler. He said, "All these things I have done since my youth," but then Jesus put His finger on his hidden idol. Jesus will do a search like nobody else can. He'll put His finger on your red button every time. He told the young man, "Sell everything you have and give it to the poor." I believe to this day that Jesus never intended for him to do that. I believe it was just an "attitude check." I think if the young man had said, "Whatever You want me to do, Jesus, I will do because I want You and You alone," that Jesus would have said, "Okay then, don't worry about selling your goods. Just follow Me. You have made it clear who your Master is."

Number 2: Those who belong to the fellowship of the uncommitted are undependable in the day of battle and endanger the lives of others.

The uncommitted are the first to cut out when it comes to spiritual warfare. They run when prayer meetings roll around, but they will be the first in line when there is a church social with spaghetti and meatballs. They suddenly find themselves busy when revival breaks out, and whenever Jesus asks them to do something, they always waver.

Why are the uncommitted so undependable? It's simple: Their hearts aren't in it. In many cases, they've never really climbed on the cross; they've just hung *around* it like casual spectators. I am convinced that when someone is genuinely born again and receives the living Christ in his heart, he or she will automatically be sold out to Christian warfare. One man who was saved during a recent revival service began to weep on my shoulder. Why? He was crying his eyes out as he interceded for his brothers and his sons to get saved. He couldn't even begin to tell you what intercession is, but he instinctively entered the battle for souls immediately. He was sold out.

The uncommitted, however, could care less about spiritual warfare. They literally endanger the lives of others. Go back to the defeat of Israel at Ai in the Book of Joshua. One man's selfish sin and lack of commitment endangered the entire Israeli army and the people of God. Why? In the day of battle, he ignored the clear instructions he had been given on what to do and what not to do. He began to steal the captured gold and hoarded up personal valuables for himself. He was undependable in the day of battle because he was uncommitted to the way of the Lord. Achan was absorbed with one thought that still plagues the church and the ministry to this day: "What can I get out of all this? What can I profit from in all of this?"

Pastor, when revival breaks out in your church, don't ever say, "What can I get out of all this?" It has nothing to do with you. It has everything to do with Jesus. Ask: "What do You want out of all this, Jesus? What do You want?"

Achan was personally responsible for the deaths of 36 innocent people who went into battle believing God was going to fight for them at Ai as He had at Jericho. If they had known about Achan's sin, they wouldn't have marched anywhere near Ai on that day. Listen friend, if you are uncommitted to Christ, do you realize how many deaths you could be responsible for? How many people have perished needlessly because of you? You break God's law every time you store up your treasures here on earth rather than storing up treasures in Heaven. You spend more time and energy on your earthly bank account than for Heaven's bank account because you constantly lust for the things of this world.

If you would spend just a little time committing yourself to the things of God, maybe your family would be saved. Maybe your son wouldn't be on drugs. Maybe!

Maybe! If the Church wasn't so laced with the fellowship of the uncommitted, maybe we would have politicians in Washington who would love Jesus and obey His Word. Maybe we would have a Congress that would open up in prayer and govern with wisdom and self-control. Who knows what kind of nation and world this would be if those of us who are so uncommitted would get committed and go after God?

Number 3:   Those who belong to the fellowship of the uncommitted often believe that God is lax in His attitude toward them.

What do you think Achan was thinking when he was stealing those forbidden goods while the other Jewish soldiers were busy in battle? Think about it. He had heard the Word of the Lord like everybody else. God said, "Don't do it!" I think he was telling himself the same thing uncommitted people say today: "Surely, God wouldn't do that. He didn't really mean it. Surely God wouldn't judge me for that." I believe Achan muttered to himself, "Come on, Joshua. Surely, you jest. It's just a little gold and silver. What are a few piddling coins to Jehovah? What does it matter in the long run?" My friend, it only takes a little bit of leaven to spread through a whole loaf. A little bit of sin will destroy your soul, and it won't take long either.

Achan must have thought God was like a man. He thought the Creator was lax in His attitude toward man. People like Achan convince themselves their good deeds will carry them through— even if they cheat here and there. "After all, God, I'm a soldier. I fought in the battle of Jericho. Surely, it's okay for me to take a little bit from these heathen people." No, friend. Achan should have known he wasn't stealing from the inhabitants of Jericho, he was stealing from God.

I've heard the uncommitted say, "God would never do that. He wouldn't really harm anyone, and I'm sure He won't punish me." I want to tell you something that I've learned about God. He is on the move, He is in a hurry, and He isn't playing games. Uncommitted people believe God is just going to "understand what they're going through." They think He will accept their flimsy excuses for not committing their all to Christ. They are dead wrong!

If you read the story of Achan in the Bible, you will discover that he was slaughtered along with every member of his family and his animals; and everything he possessed was totally destroyed. The stakes were so high that the punishment was totally devastating. Every trace of the man who dared to steal from God was wiped from the earth. God is not playing games, uncommitted person. He is very serious, and we just haven't caught on.

Number 4: **Those who belong to the fellowship of the uncommitted are nauseating to the Lord and will be judged severely for their uncommitment.**

Jesus Himself described the punishment of the uncommitted believer in the Book of Revelation. (I tell you, don't crack that book if you are uncommitted.) In His message to the church of Laodicea, Jesus held nothing back:

And unto the angel of the church of the Laodiceans write; These things saith the Amen, the faithful and true witness, the beginning of the creation of God; I know thy works, that thou art neither cold nor hot: I would thou wert cold or hot. So then because thou art lukewarm [uncommitted, in the middle, wavering, halted between two opinions, a double minded man], *and neither cold nor hot, I will spew thee out of My mouth* (Revelation 3:14-16).

I have dozens of Scriptures describing what happened to uncommitted people. It's scary. Achan was destroyed by the Lord when the people rose up and stoned Achan and his family. That man discovered the hard way that when you are uncommitted, you affect all kinds of people around you. While Achan was stealing the gold from God, his little daughter was simply playing innocently with her doll. She didn't know anything about her father's sin, but her uncommitted father caused her death. Your uncommitment to the Lord could drag your whole family into destruction too, friend.

If you indulge in a little idol worship here and a little there while your family thinks everything is fine, then on that final day your whole family will ask you, "Why didn't you tell us?" The worst nightmare I can think of is the scene of a father standing before God on Judgment Day while his little daughter screams out to him, "Daddy, what have you done? Why didn't you tell me?" Friend, uncommitment will destroy the lives of those around you.

Achan's whole family was destroyed because of his wavering heart and the sin it produced. *Achan two-timed God*, and he two-timed his family, too. It's time for *you* to make a commitment to Christ. The times are changing, and the Lord isn't putting up with uncommitment anymore. Are you part of the fellowship of the uncommitted?

Number 5: Those who belong to the fellowship of the uncommitted can switch sides.

My last point is good news. If you know that you belong to the fellowship of the uncommitted, all you have to do is decide you don't want to live like that anymore. "I don't want to be an Achan. I don't want to go down in history as a man who betrayed his God and his family for selfish idolatry. I don't want to be a black mark on my family heritage, a laughingstock and warning beacon to be pointed out as a horrible example of the wages of sin."

I have another old book in my library that dates from the 1800's. It is filled with the last sayings of ungodly men. It describes the sayings and deeds of these men during their lives and compares them to their final words as they faced the abyss of death. It is absolutely horrifying to read. Those men often screamed out like they were being dipped into hell as they crossed the veil into eternity. In the decades since that book was written, millions more have gone to hell; and for every God-denier who died, there were even more uncommitted folks who "believed" in God but insisted on "looking back." Again, the good news is that if you belong to the fellowship of the uncommitted, you can switch sides.

When Joshua reached the end of his life, and the Israelites were entering a time of rest after claiming the promised land, he warned them to avoid compromise and to commit fully to God. The Church needs to hear the same thing today:

Now therefore fear the Lord, and serve Him in sincerity and in truth: and put away the gods which your fathers served on the other side of the flood, and in Egypt; and serve ye the Lord. And if it seem evil unto you to serve the Lord, **choose you this day whom ye will serve;** *whether the gods which your fathers served that were on the other side of the flood, or the gods of the Amorites, in whose land ye dwell:* **but as for me and my house, we will serve the Lord** (Joshua 24:14-15).

The only way to *choose* a thing is to *commit* to a thing. It is time for you to choose, to make up your mind. If you're still breathing, it's not too late. You can still choose life by saying, "I am stepping out of the fellowship of the uncommitted. I'm tired of wavering, of going in and out, of the endless cycle of backsliding and getting right. I am sick of my prayers not being answered, and of hearing people ask, 'Are you a Christian?' I want people to look at me and say, 'That is an on-fire Christian who loves the Lord with all his heart, soul, and strength.' "

Cross over to the joyous fellowship of the committed. Join the band of believers who are going after God, who love Jesus with all their being, the righteous children of God. Then you can claim James 5:16b: "The effectual fervent prayer of a righteous man availeth much." May it be said of you, "When that person talks, Heaven listens."

The presence of God has a way of pressing the issue of commitment. In the old days, you could hide out in a pew and think everything was fine. In these revival services, everyone gets just a little uncomfortable at times. The committed are nudged by the Lord to greater commitment, and the uncommitted are pressed to commit or quit. God has never had any problem demanding commitment—after all, He had to commit His all to set you free. Why shouldn't He require you and me to commit everything to Him now that we are free? The glory of God is coming down on people in this revival, and no one can remain on the fence in halfway commitment when that happens.

I once prayed for a football player who had never been to this revival before. He just stood there like a statue staring at me. He was big. I asked him, "What do you think is going on around here?" He said, "I don't know." Then I said, "I will tell you what it is. God is visiting this place. Do you believe in God?" He said, "Yeah," but he was still looking at the people around him who were falling all over the place. "Do you believe He is powerful?" "Yeah." "Do you think He can deliver, heal, and set free?" "Yeah." "Have you ever seen it?" "No." "That's sad." Then I said, "I'm going to pray for you. May I pray for you?" I knew what he was going to say...and he said it: "Yeah."

I laid my hand on that guy's forehead and prayed. One of the things we established quickly in this revival was that people "fall down" under the power of God because *they can't stand up*. It's not because somebody pushed them. I knew one thing—even if I'd had the urge, I wasn't going to push this huge fellow one inch. But when the glory of God hit this young man, he was like a wet noodle. He just dropped—whomp!—straight to the ground. Then he opened his eyes again and looked up at me with a look that seemed to say, "Dear God!"

God is moving on people like this because He is covering so much territory so quickly. Revival doesn't come like a gentle rainfall; it descends like a surging, all-consuming flood. God is convincing unconvinced people like He once convinced Saul of Tarsus—in a matter of seconds. It doesn't take long to make up your mind when you're laying in the dirt and blinded by God's light. That is what is happening to thousands of people every week across the globe. God is getting a hold of people quickly. Thousands of children and teenagers are being swept into the Kingdom and fire of God today because the power of God's glory is coming down among us.

This is your opportunity to cross the line and get right with God. You may have known the Lord once, but now you have backslidden. You are in limbo, neither in nor out. Friend, that means you are totally out. Yes, God understands what you're going through—you are going through His fire. It is decision time. How long are you going to waver? When will you run out of excuses? God led you to this book because He loves you. He is ready to forgive you and wash your sins away, but first you have to choose whom you will serve.

This is a divine appointment. No matter how you ended up with this book in your hands, I can assure you this is an appointment orchestrated by God. It is time to leave the company of the wavering, the lackadaisical, the double minded, and the two-timers who betray their confession as Christians. You might be a pastor who has been shaken by God's words to Joshua, "Get off your face, and deal with the sin in the congregation." Perhaps you've been praying, "God, send revival," when He has been telling you all along, "You know one of your deacons is an adulterer. You know that man in your church is an embezzler. You know what is going on in your church, and you still want Me to send revival?"

Whether you are a pastor, a mechanic, or a successful homemaker, you need to leave the fellowship of the uncommitted now! Whatever your occupation, it is time to enter the fellowship that lives in God's presence. Revival is here and the apathy of the past will no longer do. Now is the time. This is the moment in history where you make up your mind. All it will take is for you to choose to live for Jesus. If you are serious—and I mean totally serious—about leaving the life of the uncommitted, then pray this prayer out loud with me right now, wherever you are:

Heavenly Father, I know You want me to worship and serve You alone. Lord Jesus, I am ready to lay aside every idol and shed every sin that entangles my life. Make me a soldier You can depend on in times of battle. Father, I know You are not lax concerning Your promises and commandments—please forgive me for the times I have acted like You are. I confess that I want more than anything to hear You say to me in that great day, "Well done, My good and faithful servant, in whom I am well pleased." From this day forth, I declare in Jesus' name, "As for me and my house, we will serve the Lord." Amen.

Chapter 6

God Snubs Snots

I remember the day I went to an antique shop operated by a brilliant intellectual who lived an openly homosexual lifestyle. This man was an incredible sinner. Almost the entire time I was talking to this man, he was laughing at me. He called me a fool and an idiot and said, "How can any intelligent creature believe the garbage you believe?"

I just stood there unmoved because I had an edge: God had changed my life. I had nothing to prove because God had already proven Himself to me. That man came to me "a dollar short and a day late." I had already been personally introduced to the very God he claimed didn't exist. He had a real problem, and I had a real edge. Friend, all the words and arguments in the world won't move me one inch because I've personally experienced a miraculous deliverance and salvation through Jesus Christ. My life is living proof— evidence of a God who saves lost souls. What about you?

Talk to anyone you know who has experienced divine healing. Pull out all of the clinical charts and research papers you want to. Call in every specialist you can afford and turn them loose with their case for doubt and unbelief.

Walk up to that Christian and say right in their face: "God doesn't heal." They'll just grin at you and say, "Then explain why I am standing here, healed and whole, and a whole lot happier than you are!" I have seen folks sitting in the revival services who are kissing throughout the services because God has healed their marriage. I had to tell one couple to quit necking one night after God had healed their relationship! I dare the critics and naysayers to tell that couple that God doesn't heal marriages! They would look like idiots, friend. That's like looking into a raging fire and saying, "Well, you know you'll never get heated up burning like that." The living evidence will openly destroy every claim that God doesn't exist or that He cannot heal and restore.

I felt sorry for that intellectual homosexual who ridiculed my faith. He was a brilliant man, but he was shaking his fist at God and I felt sorry for him. Then I felt the Lord release me that day to do something that I rarely do. God loved this man, and He wanted me to strike hard at the devilish ideas enslaving his soul. I looked at him and said, "Laugh if you will, but one day your knee is going to bow and your tongue is going to confess that Jesus Christ is Lord."

I said, "Look at this," and stretched out my left wrist toward him. "I want you to look at my Seiko watch and remember the date, the time, and the place. I want you to remember them because one day you will stand alone before God, and you will remember the young man who came into your antique shop and told you about Jesus. You will remember how he told you about the change in his life. You will remember how you rejected Him."

I pulled back my wrist and the man's eyes continued to follow the watch. Then he let out a fake laugh that was calculated to sound hideous. You know how sinners will often laugh just to cover up their embarrassment or shame. This man was desperately trying to cover up the fact that he had been seriously affected by God's wake-up call.

We often talk about stubborn sinners like this man (and I used to be a stubborn sinner too), but we have some stubborn sinners right in our own churches and homes. One of them might even be *you*. The only way to know is to have a heart checkup.

*From whence come wars and fightings among you? come they not hence, even of your lusts that war in your members? Ye lust, and have not: ye kill, and desire to have, and cannot obtain: ye fight and war, yet ye have not, because ye ask not. Ye ask, and receive not, because ye ask amiss, that ye may consume it upon your lusts. Ye adulterers and adulteresses, know ye not that the friendship of the world is enmity with God? whosoever therefore will be a friend of the world is the enemy of God. Do ye think that the scripture saith in vain, The spirit that dwelleth in us lusteth to envy? But He giveth more grace. Wherefore He saith, **God resisteth the proud, but giveth grace unto the humble**. Submit yourselves therefore to God. Resist the devil, and he will flee from you* (James 4:1-7).

There are only two points to this message, and they are both found in a single verse: "God resisteth the proud, but giveth grace unto the humble" (Jas. 4:6). This *may* be ridiculously simple for some of you, but it is profound. This verse is simple and direct—you don't need a Greek lexicon or a degree in biblical languages to understand what it means. In fact, it is so simple that we usually miss it: God resisteth the *proud*, but giveth grace to the *humble*. Ask yourself one question: Who is James talking to?

I wish this verse was only aimed at stone-cold sinners, but it isn't. I wish it didn't apply to anyone in the Body of Christ, *but it does*. Friend, it is important for you to open your heart to God's Word and allow the Holy Spirit to speak to you in any way He wants. Now I am an evangelist, so I'm obliged to make my first point simple and direct.

Point Number 1: *God snubs snots.*

If you have followed the Brownsville Revival at all, then you probably know that I try to preach a balanced word each week. Sometimes I preach sweet "Twinkie" messages on God's tender love for the sinner and His grace to the believer, because that is in the Bible. I also preach the "other side" of the gospel of Jesus Christ. I preach the truth about Judgment Day and even on the forgotten and sometimes forbidden topic of hellfire (because that is in the Word too). I call these kinds of messages "brussel sprouts." This chapter on "God Snubs Snots" leans more toward the brussel sprouts category.

According to the Bible, Christians who qualify as "snots" have a lot to worry about. I love that word. Do you want to know why? You see "snots" everywhere you go in America—you can almost smell a snot when he's coming. If you go to a mall, you're paying a visit to "Snotsville." Snobs and snots are lurking everywhere you go. Snobs are starchy. They reek of arrogance. They think they are God's gift to mankind. But friend, you are a pain to be around because you think you know everything. You think you have it all together, but you're wrong. God is against you."

James tells us that God resists the proud and gives grace to the humble, and in Psalm 138:6, the psalmist says: "Though the Lord be high, yet hath He respect unto the lowly: but the proud He knoweth afar off." I don't want to live as a proud man. I don't want God to look at me from a distance; I want Him to draw close to me in intimate fellowship. That is why I want to avoid qualifying for the category of folks described in James 4:6: **God *resisteth the proud.***

God sets Himself against the proud and the haughty. Listen, if you are humble before God, then you have nothing to worry about. But if you're not (and most of us fall short in this area from time to time), then you may be a religious snob, and God snubs snots. The word *snub* describes God's attitude and actions toward the proud. It means "to treat with contempt or neglect"[1] and "to treat with scorn...disdain, etc.; to behave coldly toward."[2] When God does it, it means "to resist, to rebuke." If you see somebody look at you, shake their heads in apparent disgust, and then pointedly turn away from you, then you've been snubbed.

Have you resisted God's gentle wooing or disregarded His commands? If you could see Him, would you see Him smile with joy or shake His head in disappointment and disgust? Worst of all, would you see Him turn away from you and lay aside your prayers (if there are any)? If the answer is yes, then *you have been snubbed, you snot!*

Too many of us in the Church smell like that nasty cheese you find in the larger grocery stores—Limburger cheese. We stink in the nostrils of God. Others just spend too much time around people who are a stench to God. They will tell you, "God doesn't heal, God doesn't deliver, God doesn't move on people like they say in Brownsville, and other parts of the world. That couldn't be God, because we have God in a little box at our church, and He doesn't do anything like that in *our church*, don't you see?"

God hates pride with an unquenchable hatred. Some of you have never received anything from God because you reek of pride. It is only His loving mercy that is withholding His judgment on your pride problem. In your worst moments, you may think you are resisting Him, but He left your side a long time ago. He is busy drawing close to the humble.

What is a *snot*? A snot is "a stuck up, in-your-face, know-it-all, got-it-figured-out, high-minded, arrogant, stuck-on-self, fast-talking, smooth-walking, God-rejecting, pitiful human being." A snot is a snob whose attitude is offensively superior.

The fashion industry absolutely loves snobs. In fact, you will find a phrase in the dictionary that was coined by the fashion industry called "snob appeal." I hope you haven't been suckered into it. I'm not kidding about the dictionary listing. According to *Merriam-Webster's Collegiate Dictionary*, *snob appeal* means "qualities of a product that appeal to the snobbery in a purchaser."[3] Snobs love products with high prices and tags from foreign countries. This is important for genuine snob appeal. A true snob will walk into a store and say, "Give me something imported. I want an Italian suit. Not that one, it's too cheap. Give me that one—that will put old So-and-So in their proper place. They don't make that much in a month."

That's snob appeal. I've lived in some of the countries where most of the "snob clothes" are made. I've toured the factories and watched workers make a shirt for $3.49 that Saks Fifth Avenue will sell to snobs for $79.00. Then I watched those workers take the *same shirt* to another table, and sew on white K-mart buttons. That way K-mart can sell that $3.49 shirt for $14.95 to average people who can't afford to be snobs.

My friend in Costa Rica took me to the "tag and button room" in his factory where all this takes place. I said, "You've got to be kidding." He said, "No, here are 2,000 mauve Oxford shirts ready for shipment, to be sold in department stores." Then he showed me the boxes filled with the unique brand tags and special buttons for the New York batch. I guess those buttons were pretty valuable, because all it took was a few buttons from the snob box to instantly raise the price of a shirt $50.

Satan runs the same scam on Christians. Let me ask you this: *Where do you go to church?* Do you go to "First Church"? What is the first thing you tell people about your church? "We have 275 people in our choir. Of course, we are getting rid of our old choir robes, and we're going to change the color of the carpet. It's already two years old." Snobbery in the church will price the gospel beyond the reach of the very people who need it. That is why Jesus was found among the outcasts more often than in the temple with the Pharisees. My friend, religion will damn your soul to hell. As I've said many times in this revival, religion is hanging around the cross, but Christianity is getting on the cross. Religion is for snots; Christianity is for the humble. I am concerned because America is a religious nation, not a Christian nation.

My friend, if you are pastoring a church with snob appeal, dump it. Purge the snob from your church. Pastor a church that will minister to the hurting and the dying—even if it has to get its hands dirty doing it. Pastor a church that will be a hospital where anyone and everyone who longs to be whole will be welcome. I promise you, pastor, if a snob leaves, you are better off! I'm an evangelist, but my wife and I have also planted and pastored churches for years. I've had to deal with it all.

The joy of planting a church is working with all of the brand-new people who are hungry for God. The problem is that a lot of them will try to come in and attempt to take control with their money or influence. If you are desperate, you may become susceptible to snob appeal. Inevitably, the snobs will come in and start pumping in big offerings just as you begin to build a new church building to accommodate the growing crowds, and naturally you need this money. Suddenly you will find a $50,000 donation in the offering, but there is a long, break-resistant string attached to that check that will often times lead you to a snot. Don't be surprised if he slides up beside you, takes your hand like he's doing you a favor, and says with an air of authority, "Oh pastor, I want to let you know where I'd like that money to go...."

God will resist you if you are living for self, if you are always seeking to please men, and if you are a lover of pleasure and the things of this world. The cure for a snot is repentance on bended knee. You also need to drop to your knees if you find yourself unable or unwilling to receive a word of correction or rebuke—even though you know you deserve it.

You also need to repent before God if you know you have an exaggerated estimate of your own strength. Robert Murray McCheyne used to say, "Nothing is more deceitful than a man's estimate of his own strength."

Another sign of dangerous pride is the habit of constantly judging the character and conduct of others. That means you think that you are "God's plan for man." Do you sit back in the pew and judge everything? We constantly hear criticism from people who claim to know everything about this revival and have never been here! These people have even written papers on the revival "sight unseen." I remember when someone in a newspaper article said that people weren't getting saved. At that time, the revival had been going for three solid months, and I thought, *That's a dumb thing to say.* I looked at the hundreds of people sitting in the auditorium whom we personally prayed with and led to the Lord and just shook my head. At this point more than 100,000 souls have been saved in this revival, and that is a conservative number because it is our habit to cut our actual count by half just to preserve integrity and avoid any appearance of evil.

Point Number 2: *God hugs the humble.*

God snubs snots, but I have good news. The second half of James 4:6 tells us, in essence, that *God hugs the humble.* James put it in more formal terms when he wrote that God "...giveth grace to the humble" (Jas. 4:6). In verse 10, James says, "Humble [thyself] in the sight of the Lord, and He shall lift you up." True humility does not require you to "think lowly of yourself." That's not the point, friend. It means you should think rightly and truthfully about yourself. Almost every night pastors come forward and repent of the sin in their lives and make a fresh start—that is true humility. God can bless that, but He cannot bless the snob who is living in sin but nevertheless sits there with a pastor's badge on his lapel thinking, *I can't go up there because I'm a pastor.*

The great evangelist George Whitefield read a book in the 1700's called *The Life of God and the Soul of Man*. It led him to surrender his heart to Christ, and it changed his life. That book was written by a young man named Henry Scougal. Young Henry once told his students, "If I had printed on the wall everything that your mind thought over the last few days, you would crawl out of this building!" Scougal was a teacher at a Bible school at the age of 18. The writings of this powerful man of God were what brought George Whitefield to a saving knowledge of Jesus Christ. Remember: *The flower of humility always grows on the grave of pride*. If you want God's grace, then you must humble yourself. Dethrone yourself and put God in His rightful position.

One Christian minister shared, "Pastors, I was never of any use until I found out that God did not intend for me to be a great man." I love that. He just wants us to be a bunch of nobodies working for Him, and not taking a drop of His glory. That's humility. I've seen some great men who were humble servants in my time.

I've already described the impact Brother Leonard Ravenhill made on my life, but there are others. One man was David Wilkerson, and another is a man named Carlos Anacondia from Argentina. He is the most humble man I have ever met in my life. He is very simple by choice. When some people wanted to write a book and compose songs about him, he wouldn't even allow an interview with them. He doesn't care about himself. Why are people so interested in Carlos? Brother Anacondia has led over one million people to Jesus in Argentina alone.

I have seen Carlos Anacondia walk before a crowd of thousands and wave his hand across the crowd in the name of Jesus, and every demon-possessed and demon-oppressed person in that meeting would begin to convulse and fall to the ground under the power of God! Carlos doesn't speak English; he preaches and prays in Spanish, but whether he is ministering in South America or North America, I want to tell you the devil knows what he is saying. I've watched him wave his hand over a crowd of 20,000 to 25,000 people under the unction of the Holy Ghost and I've witnessed thousands being hit by the power of God!

Carlos has become well known and revered in Latin America, Europe, and other areas of the world. Despite all of that, I promise you that if Carlos walked into your home, your office, or your workplace, you would never know him or pick him out of a crowd because he is so genuinely humble. Do you know what he would do after an evening service if he was here? He would go out to the waffle house and have an omelet—he's not interested in expensive restaurants, plush hotel rooms, and private meetings with bigwigs. He cares about souls.

Don't talk to me about the blessings you want from God. Look at people like this man and think, *Maybe I could lead over one million people to Jesus if I was rock bottom like this man*. In the years I was with him, I never saw or heard Carlos take a drop of glory from God. Everything was, "Praise the Lord; bless the Lord; God healed you; God saved you: Give Him the praise—Carlos Anacondia didn't do anything."

God resists the proud, but He gives grace (that is His favor) to the humble. I think that one of the reasons this revival is being blessed is because no one on the platform wants anything but Jesus. You will have a problem with this message if you once came to Jesus and lived for

God, but then rose up one day and said just like satan before you, "I can do this on my own. I don't need church. I can do this." The driving force behind a snot is pride, and satan is the chief snot.

Satan was a Sunday school boy. He was in church all his life. He is a "backslidden church member," the first one who said, "I can do this on my own. In fact, I'm going to rise up and be like the Most High." He was also the first being in all of creation to fail. I've lost count of the many people I have talked to who made the same mistake. Time and again, people come to this revival after being away from God for months, after backsliding because of pride. They come in here and weep at this altar after discovering they *can't* do it on their own. Friend, you need every gift, every spiritual weapon, every tool, and every provision God has for you—including the vital support, training, and protection provided by the local church.

If you have been a snot and you want it to stop, then begin by stripping yourself of that pride. Don't let lucifer, the king of pride, take you down to his level. Pride took him down in the beginning, and it will take him all the way down to the bottom in God's timing. The devil wants to drag you down too. Pride is satan's big flagship. If God is working in your life, respond to Him now, in this moment. Do not delay until some unimportant detail distracts you from something far more important. Come back to Him today. If you have never known the Lord and you want to find out what true life is all about, remember our text: "God resisteth the proud, but giveth grace to the humble" (Jas. 4:6b). He is waiting to meet you on your knees and enfold you in His love.

If you cringed because you knew those descriptions of a snot fit you, then I want to remind you that it isn't too late to turn your life around. You can do it right now, right where you are. If you are serious about breaking free of your snotty ways, then pray this prayer out loud:

Dear Jesus, thank You for still speaking to me, even though I know I've been a snot. Please forgive me for the times I stole Your glory before men, or boasted I could make it on my own without Your help. I repent of my sins and I acknowledge my complete dependence upon You. I ask You to forgive me, because I have sinned against You and I have hurt You and others. Please forgive me, Jesus, and wash away my sins. I ask You to be my Savior, my Lord, and my very best friend. I commit myself to You 100 percent. From this moment on, I will humbly follow You, Lord Jesus. In Your precious name I pray, Lord Jesus. Amen.

Endnotes

1. *Merriam-Webster's Collegiate Dictionary*, 10th ed., p. 1113.

2. *Webster's New Universal Unabridged Dictionary*, 2nd ed. (New York, NY: Simon & Schuster, 1983), p. 1720.

3. *Merriam-Webster's Collegiate Dictionary*, 10th ed., p. 1112.

Chapter 7

Lucifer's List

I often mention the years I spent in Argentina, working around godly men like Carlos Anacondia who have led millions to Jesus over the last ten years or so. Jeri and I were there from 1985 to 1992, and we will never forget the things we saw during those great revival campaigns. One of the most unusual things about these meetings was the "demon tent" that was set up immediately behind the platform.

There is a lot of spiritism in Argentina, which is due, in part, to the thousands and thousands of cults and occultic sects that moved into that nation when it became a democracy and opened its doors to foreign nations and travelers. They just flooded the country. One of these was the Makumba witchcraft cult that moved in from Brazil along with its devilish practice of human sacrifice. At that time thousands of Argentineans became hopelessly bound by the devil.

When Brother Anacondia would wave his hand across the crowd, rebuking the devil, hundreds of people all over the audience would begin to drop like flies, screaming out for deliverance. We saw this happen night after night for eight years. Many of these victims had fallen under demonic control during their childhood, perhaps after dabbling with witchcraft or some other form of the occult. Someone would stand next to them and wave a handkerchief in the air, and ushers would come to carry them away to the "demon or deliverance tent." Hundreds of ushers worked these campaigns in teams that would pick up the people and take them to the tent as they were kicking and screaming. Everything imaginable went on inside that tent, friend. People were pulling out their eyes, ripping their flesh, tearing off their clothes, and shouting out, "I'm the Christ. I am the Christ." Others would call out in the name of the devil.

A friend of mine who pastors a large church in America came down to visit us, and he watched all of this going on. He was okay until Carlos began binding devils. He watched as nearly 500 demon-possessed people were ushered into the demon tent. You could hear the warfare going on inside the tent. It was a bit eerie, but it was merely the sound of people being delivered from demonic oppression and possession.

I turned to my friend and said, "Do you want to go in with me? Come on, let's go." He shook his head and said, "No way. I'm not going in there." I looked at him and said, "But brother, you're a pastor of a large congregation. You've got a great church in America." He said, "I'll tell you right now, Steve. I might have a great church in America, but I could never take on anything like that. There is sin in my life, man. There is sin in my life. I'm not right with God. I could not go into that tent." Why did this pastor say what he did? He said it because he knew the Scriptures, particularly the journal of the New Testament church in the Book of the Acts of the Apostles.

And God was performing extraordinary miracles by the hands of Paul, so that handkerchiefs or aprons were even carried from his body to the sick, and the diseases left them and the evil spirits went out. But also some of the Jewish exorcists, who went from place to place, attempted to name over those who had the evil spirits the name of the Lord Jesus, saying, "I adjure you by the Jesus whom Paul preaches." And seven sons of one Sceva, a Jewish chief priest, were doing this. And the evil spirit answered and said to them, "I recognize Jesus, and I know about Paul, but who are you?" And the man, in whom was the evil spirit, leaped on them and subdued all of them and overpowered them, so that they fled out of that house naked and wounded. And this became known to all, both Jews and Greeks, who lived in Ephesus; and fear fell upon them all and the name of the Lord Jesus was being magnified (Acts 19:11-17 NAS).

Paul the apostle said, "Nevertheless, the firm foundation of God stands having this seal, *'The Lord knows those who are His'* " (2 Tim. 2:19a NAS). Compare this with the demonic challenge issued to the sons of Sceva: "I recognize Jesus, and I know about Paul, but who are you?"

Everybody wants their name written down in glory, but I want my name somewhere else too. I want my name on a list that causes all hell to look up. Leonard Ravenhill used to say to me over and over again, "Steve, I don't care if you're known from coast to coast. I don't care if they know you from England to Scotland to China to Los Angeles, or from Canada to Mexico. It makes no difference if you are headline news across the country or the world. All that matters, Steve, is this: *Are you known in hell?*" Friend, do they know you down there? Do they talk about you in hell? Does the devil get up in the morning and get a bowl of grits and put hot sauce all over it and begin thinking about you? And as soon as you get out of bed, does he go, "Oh my God, he's up"? *Are you known in hell?*

My pastor friend discovered that night in Argentina that his name was not on lucifer's list. He suddenly saw his hidden sin, and he knew that if he walked into the "demon tent" he might hear the words: "I recognize Jesus, and I know about Paul, but who are you?" He was afraid those spirits would come all over him.

Many good people from mainline denominations really don't believe in talking about the devil or demons, but I urge them to once again read the New Testament. *Jesus spent His three years of adult ministry rebuking them.* He talked to demons, and He cast them out with no mercy. Demons didn't disappear after Calvary. What do you think has America so bound up? What do you think is causing our teenagers to stick needles into their arms in an unprecedented "revival" of heroin use? Why is heroin becoming the number one drug in America once again? The devil has seen to it that the price of heroin has dropped to five dollars a "hit" or dose. Kids can use their lunch money to get a hit of heroin—and they do! Our drug problem stems from a far more sinister and powerful source than a bunch of folks in Colombia.

Paul said, "For we wrestle not against flesh and blood..." (Eph. 6:12). There is an evil spirit world that is trying to destroy this nation. There is a spirit trying to destroy Norway; there is a malignant evil spirit trying to destroy Germany; and there is an unclean spirit trying to destroy England. We need to stand up in Jesus' name and declare: "I'm telling you now, satan, in Jesus' name you aren't going to do it. You aren't going to do it!"

There is power and authority in the name of Jesus. There is deliverance and healing in that name. Anyone who has ever been delivered from demonic bondage can testify to that. I know I can. I remember the time one of my old friends came up to me right after I got saved, and said, "You're just using Jesus as a crutch." I'd been powerfully delivered from drug and alcohol addiction, so I said, "Crutch? He's my wheelchair too, man. He's everything to me. I couldn't walk, talk, breathe, or do anything without Jesus. He's *everything* to me. What are you talking about? Crutch? I *am* a cripple. I *was* crippled in sin. I was beaten down and wasted, but Jesus came and lifted me up, man. He's everything to me." That guy said, "All right. All right. All right." Why? Because he was expecting me to bow my head and go, "No, He's not my crutch. I can make it on my own, man." No, friend. Don't say things like that to me.

The morning before I first preached this message in the Brownsville Revival, the Lord woke me up at 5:30 a.m. to give me this poem:

Lucifer's List

There is a list, my friend. Hear it well, that is
      penned in red in the pits of hell.
It contains the name of a chosen few. "Jesus, I
      know, but who are you?"
This list of names is a horror, you see, to the
      demons of darkness; they have to flee.
From those who are written down in this book,
      they run so fast, not a second look.

These people are classified all by name. It all
      began when to Christ they came.
Came to the cross, looked in His face, repented
      of sins, received His grace.
It all began to make sense that day. Convicted of
      sin, something's in the way.

Between God and man, great distance be. Who'll
    close the gap for you and me?

His Son was sent, His Blood was shed, for
    without the Blood, the Bible said,
There would be no pardon for mortal man. A
    life must be given. It was God's plan.
On that fateful day the die was cast. The Lamb
    of God would be the last,
The last to bleed upon the ground. But for the
    sins of man it would be sound.

The Blood, it dripped. The drops were heard. In
    the corridors of hell, not a word.
They trembled, they shook, as the cry came out,
    "Forgive them, Father." Then came the shout,
    "Eli, Eli, lama sabachthani?"
    He pierced the heavens with that fateful cry.
"My God, My God, Why hast Thou forsaken Me,"
    were the words of Jesus, hanging on the tree.

Those words rang out for all to hear. The Son of
    God He loved so dear.
Sin separates, divides, keeps us from Him. But
    now the gap was closing in.
The demons shook; what they feared the most
    was now reality to that cringing host.
The Lamb of God had opened the way
    for you and me on that blessed day.

He died, was carried to the tomb, but He only
    borrowed that vacant room.
For in three days, He would arise, with the keys of
    hell, fire in His eyes.
Time went by, and a man named Saul was struck
    by God in the sight of all.

He cried out, "What do I do?" That's all that
    mattered, his life was through.

Now he played a different part, a man of God,
    Christ in his heart.
He blazed the trail, leading men to God. Hell
    took notes while the road he trod.
There came a day when Sceva's seven sons were
    playing games with the Holy One.
They used His name like a wind-up key hoping
    to score, win the victory.

The demons laughed, they roared in hell at
    those foolish men. They knew them well—
Not as men of God, soldiers of the cross, but as
    fools who played with the name of God.
Yes, there is a list, my friend. Hear it well, that's
    penned in red in the pits of hell.
It contains the names of the chosen few. "Jesus,
    I know, but who are you?"

Be a part, my friend, of this famous book,
the one down there, please take a look.
Are you written down? Better know it well.
It's lucifer's list. Are you known in hell?

Let me ask you one of the most important questions
in life: *Who are you?* Your answer will reveal a lot about
where you stand with God and your destiny. Will you tell
me, "Well, Brother Steve, I'm a stockbroker. I've been
raised in a good, upper-middle class home. My dad was
a good man— God rest his soul. He was a successful car
dealer. My mom raised four boys and three girls on
her own when my dad died. I have fought all my life to
get to where I am today. I've paid my dues, and now I'm

reaping the benefits. I'm a good husband, a good father, and a good provider for my family. That's who I am"?

No, friend, that's not who you are. That is who you *say* you are, and what you do. It is time to get a grip on who you really are. Young person, you're not just a kid in school. You may tell me, "I'm Michelle. I'm 18 years old, and I'm going to graduate this year. I've done well in school, and my mom and dad both have honor roll bumper stickers on the car. I'm heading off to Florida State in Tallahassee next year to pursue a career in teaching. Basically, I'm a good person. I'm a decent girl with a good future." Sorry, friend, that's not who you are. That's what you do.

On the other hand, you might tell me, "Well, Steve, I'm sort of a wash-out in life. Somebody gave me this book. I guess they thought I was what you might call a rebellious person. I'm from a rough home filled with divorce, anger, and hatred. For the last several years I've just been drinking, smoking dope, and hanging out. I come from nowhere, and I'm going nowhere." No, friend. That's not who you are. That is what you're doing with your life, but that's not who you are.

Everybody has an opinion about themselves. When I was a drug addict, I was a hot shot. I used to boast, "It's my life. I can do what I want." How many young people have said that to their parents?

Everyone has an opinion about themselves. What about the seven sons of Sceva? What kind of people were they? They were messing around and dabbling in sorcery. The King James Version of the Bible says they were "vagabonds," which means that they were wanderers. History tells us that during this time, that area of the world was full of so-called exorcists, interpreters of dreams, fortune tellers, charmers, and masters of the black arts. It reminds me of modern-day America with its thriving TV psychic business and fascination with the occult.

What would happen if the sons of Sceva could share their own personal testimony with us today? Would one of them say, "Before this experience, I was a successful witch doctor who made money in black magic"? Maybe another would say, "I've always been a pretty sharp guy who could figure out things in my mind. We've been able to perform some pretty interesting feats in front of the crowds in Ephesus. But that day was different...." Every one of them would have a testimony, friend.

Who do you think you are? That is a good question; now let me ask you another one: *Who do other people say you are?* Do they say you're a great preacher or pastor? That's a scary thing to hear. When someone says you're a great preacher, don't listen to it because the weather will change. That same person may come back to you the next day and tell you to move into another profession. All you have to do is begin to walk on their toes with the Word of God, and their opinions will change with the speed of light.

Who do others say that you are? "Well, he's a wonderful man. He's a great father. She's a Proverbs 31 wife and mother. He's an incredible left-handed pitcher. She's a straight-A student. He's the most powerful preacher I've ever heard. He's just a great guy. Everything about him is so wonderful. He's so smart. He's a Methodist. He's a Baptist. He's a Greek Orthodox. He is a Messianic Jew." Who are people saying that you are, friend? Beware friend, because the opinions of others don't have anything to do with reality either.

Maybe there were people hanging around the sons of Sceva who said, "If anybody can cast out a demon, these boys can. Call the sons of Sceva. They can do it." Friend, don't listen to the words of men—whether those words are positive or negative.

Who do you think you are? Who do other people say you are? Neither one of those matter, friend. What really matters is my last question: *Who is the real you?* There are four types of people who come to this revival. In the first category are those people who are *close to the truth*, like the Ethiopian eunuch. God sent Philip to intercept this man who was reading from the scroll of Isaiah while traveling down a road. Philip jumped on the chariot and led the man to Jesus. This man and those like him are close to the truth.

Then there are people here who are *distant from the truth*, like the Samaritan woman who met Jesus at the well in Samaria. She was as lost as a goose in a snowstorm. She didn't know what was going on. Sometimes these people come in to mock or make fun of the things of God. Many of the witches who have come into our revival services were far from the truth, and they have been known to sit in the back and chant their curses—that is until several of them got saved. They had underestimated the power of the living God.

A third group is comprised of people who *have known the truth and have backslidden*. Like the prodigal son, they were once in a good situation and were in relationship with the Lord, but they drifted away. The last category of people have *heard the truth, have been set free, and are living in victory*. I pray that you are in this group. However, when it comes to the soul-hungry demons of hell, there are only two groups of people: those who know the Lord and those who don't.

We have already considered what the seven sons of Sceva would tell us in our day, but what would happen if we hauled in the demon-possessed man who beat Sceva's sons senseless? What would happen if you walked past this chained demoniac? What would his demons say to you—would they see you as a threat or would they laugh at you? Would they say, "Jesus, I know, and Paul I know. But who on earth are you? You have no authority"? Would they spot your hidden sin and call you a hypocrite, friend?

There is a list in hell and I want to be on it. If you are a Blood-washed, on-fire, justified, God-seeking, interceding, Spirit-filled, hell-gate-shaking, frontline warrior for Jesus, then you are known in hell. You are on lucifer's list—hell's roll of fear and Heaven's roll of honor. Your goal in life should be to make lucifer's list, not to live the lukewarm life of a pretend Christian.

Do you want to be on lucifer's list? Make sure you have been genuinely converted like Paul the apostle. Allow Jesus Christ to wash away your sins with His Blood. The Bible says, "Therefore if any man be in Christ, he is a new creature: old things are passed away; behold, all things are become new" (2 Cor. 5:17). Let the Lord regenerate you and make you brand new.

If you are backslidden, the way to get on lucifer's list is to "front-slide." Get rid of the sin in your life by repenting of your sins. Get right with God. The demons knew Paul because he was holy and on fire for God. They knew him on a first-name basis because he was consecrated and untouchable in Christ. He said, "Yea doubtless, and I count all things but loss for the excellency of the knowledge of Christ Jesus my Lord: for whom I have suffered the loss of all things, and do count them but dung, that I may win Christ" (Phil. 3:8). Paul was not only converted, he was consecrated. How about you?

Are you consecrated, set apart to Jesus Christ, or are you dedicated to everything else? If a demon-possessed man was ushered into your room, would you be powerless? You can look at a demon-possessed man and say, "In the name of Martin Luther..." or "In the name of Charles Wesley..." and even "In the name of Brownsville Assembly, in the name of the Pentecostal Union, in the name of the Assemblies of God, and in the name of the Southern Baptists...." It won't do any good—the demons in that man wouldn't even blink an eye in fear. That stuff doesn't mean a hill of beans to the powers of darkness. It never has and it never will. On the other hand, if you are a Blood-washed, holy, sin-hating, God-fearing, Holy Ghost-filled man or woman of God, and if you look at that demon and say, "In the name of Jesus...," then all hell will shake!

Lucifer has a list, and one name above every name heads that list of mighty warriors of renown. His name is Jesus, and the demons of darkness can't stand that name. They hate it when another name is added to the list of unbeatable foes under Jesus' name. I can imagine what it was like the day Saul of Tarsus was on his way to Damascus to kill some Christians, friend. I can almost see the secretary of hell sitting at his desk with a red hot pen in his hand and flames licking up all around him. As he observed Saul of Tarsus begin his murderous mission, the demons around him were talking about Saul, saying, "We got our man, just look at him go. He's ripping the Church apart!"

Then they saw their man suddenly thrown to the ground—Wham!—in broad daylight! The corridors of hell must have buzzed with alarm, "Did you see that? What's going on?!" Hoards of demons were dispatched to investigate, but within a split second, they were bound and powerless as they were kept back by the great field of God's glory. The Holy Ghost had descended upon Saul of Tarsus, and he was transformed in a matter of seconds. Only a few seconds earlier, he had been breathing hateful curses and forming vile plans to destroy the redeemed of God.

When Saul's face turned toward Heaven and he said, "What would You have me to do, Lord?" the shaken secretary of hell reached down with a feeble hand and a red hot pen to write another name on that hated list of lucifer's: P-A-U-L. Immediately the orders went out, "Stop him! Stop him!" Suddenly the eager demons put their tails between their legs and said, "Paul? Oh no, sir. Don't you know his eyes burn like fire, and his forehead is like a flint." The Bible says Paul spent the rest of his days talking about Jesus Christ and the power of God. I guarantee you those demons took down his name and underlined it again and again and again! The chief demons kept ordering the citizens of hell, "After him! After him!" but nothing can stop a Holy Ghost-filled man! That man wrote letter after letter to the churches in Rome, Corinth, Galatia, Ephesus, and Philippi. Nobody could stop a Blood-washed man who was known in hell.

What kind of life do you want to live? Do you want to make a difference in this life? The only way you will make a difference is if your name is written down on lucifer's list. Those are the only people who count, friend. The devil knows if you know Jesus.

Who do you think you are? Who do others say that you are? Are you known in hell as one of the Blood-washed names on lucifer's list? Are you a bold soldier of the cross? I was in a restaurant in New Jersey one time with a man who asked the waitress, "Ma'am, before we order this meal, we just want to ask you a question: Do you know Jesus Christ as your personal Savior?" That waitress suddenly gasped and said, "Oh, my God!" Then she put her hands over her face, fell on the floor, and repented of her sins. That very morning she had prayed, "God, if You're out there, send somebody my way to tell me."

Your name needs to be on two important lists, friend. First, your name had better be written in the Lamb's Book of Life. Second, if you want to make a real difference in this life, then your name also needs to be on lucifer's list. It doesn't matter what other people think. It doesn't even matter what you say about yourself—are you known in hell? Are you clean and spotless before God, and blameless before satan's taunting demons? "I recognize Jesus, and I know about Paul...." Are you known in hell? If you want to be known and feared in hell, my friend—if you want to be on lucifer's list, then you need to be right with God. Pray this prayer out loud with me right now:

Lord Jesus, I thank You for saving my soul and giving me eternal life. I want to make a real difference in this life. Make me a Blood-washed, Holy Ghost-filled, Bible-quoting, demon-defeating warrior of the cross. I refuse to hide any sin or fault from You. Please wash me clean in Your precious Blood. Anoint me to boldly declare Your name in places of darkness for Your glory. I want my name to be on lucifer's list below Your name and those of Paul, Peter, and millions of Your other faithful followers. I acknowledge again that You are my Savior, my Lord, and my very best friend. I commit myself to You 100 percent, and I will humbly follow You, Lord Jesus. In Your precious name I pray. Amen.

Chapter 8

Pulled From the Fire

When I was a little boy, I went out to a field with my older brother on Thanksgiving Day. I always looked up to my brother, and I thought he was a genius. We walked out to the middle of a five-acre field, and we were almost invisible in the high, brown grass. We were trying to bide our time while waiting for the call to eat a big Thanksgiving dinner. Matches and little boys are always a bad combination, and this day was no exception. We stamped a small circle in the grass. Then we piled up some dry grass in the middle of the circle and lit a match. I'll never forget what happened.

Right after we lit that little pile of grass, a gust of wind blew through, and within seconds that field was ablaze! It quickly spread toward the houses in the neighborhood. First an entire acre was on fire, and then *we* were in danger too. We flew back to our house and ran up the stairway straight to our room. The rest of the family was busy preparing the Thanksgiving dinner, and the smell of the roast turkey had filled the house. This must have masked the overpowering smell of smoke coming from our clothes.

We ran into that room, shut the door, pulled out our building blocks, and started to play like we had been there all day. You can probably guess what happened after that. We heard the sound of sirens in the distance—seven different alarms were sounded that Thanksgiving morning at 11 o'clock. It was time for us to go down and eat turkey, and George and I were afraid to come out from our hiding place. We were too afraid to look out the window or go downstairs to find out what was happening to the fire.

It took the firemen several hours to get the blaze under control, but in the end there was no damage to existing structures. At that point, weary policemen and firemen began to go from door to door, asking parents, "Do you know anything about this blaze? Do you have any children at home?" I still remember when they came to our house in full uniform. "Yes, ma'am, sorry to disturb you. Are you familiar with the fire down the road? We are still putting it out, but we just want to find out if there are any young people or any children who might have been down in that vicinity who could have possibly started it."

I can still hear my mother saying, "No, my boys have been in the bedroom. George, Steve?" she called. "Do you know anything about that fire?" Desperate, we lied through our teeth. "No, Mom. Not us." The fire was in the newspaper the next day. It was a big blaze that was remembered by many for years.

Nearly 30 years later, Jeri and I were working as missionaries building churches in Argentina. My mother came down to visit us, and as we were just talking one day, that fire came to my mind. I looked at Mama and remembered how she stood up for George and me that day, "Not my boys, not my kids, no. They weren't even outside. They have been in the house all day." I took a deep breath and said, "Mama, I need to talk to you about something." She hated to hear me say that. I had been living for God for over 15 years, but she still hated to hear me say, "I need to talk to you about something." She knew it was a signal that I was going to confess to one of those crimes that her boy would never have done.

I said, "Mama, you remember that Thanksgiving Day?" This time it was too much, and she interrupted me, "Dear God, don't say it, Steve...." Mama refused to believe that one for a while. I'll never forget the Thanksgiving Day George and I learned about the power of a pack of matches. Since then, I've discovered that sin is a lot like fire.

But, beloved, remember ye the words which were spoken before of the apostles of our Lord Jesus Christ; how that they told you there should be mockers in the last time, who should walk after their own ungodly lusts. These be they who separate themselves, sensual, having not the Spirit. But ye, beloved, building up yourselves on your most holy faith, praying in the Holy Ghost, keep yourselves in the love of God, looking for the mercy of our Lord Jesus Christ unto eternal life. And of some have compassion, making a difference: and others save with fear, pulling them out of the fire; hating even the garment spotted by the flesh (Jude 1:17-23).

I recently awoke with this Scripture on my heart. I sense an urgency because I perceive an incredible danger waiting to consume many believers across this land. This urgency is the first point of this message: *Too many in the Body of Christ are suffering from the consequences of living too close to the fires of hell.* Others have fallen headlong into the devil's bonfire and are at the point of death. Sin looks enticing. Is it possible that you, too, caught a good glimpse of the fire and are beginning to move towards it? You see the inviting flames dancing in the darkness of night, and you may be drawn to it just as a moth is drawn to a flame. I have learned a little bit about the fiery nature of sin and its damning effects on individuals. That is why I preach the way I do.

The day before I preached this message at the Brownsville Revival, I wrote a poem entitled, "The Devil's Bonfire." Beware friend, you may well begin to sense what is happening in your own life.

The Devil's Bonfire

"Play with me my little friend, our time together
    will never end.
I'll give you just a taste right now to warm your
    toes, to make you smile.
Come here, come close, don't be afraid of this
    little fire that I have made.
It's cozy and warm, draw near and see; don't
    walk away, no need to flee.
That's good, sit down right here by me; into
    your eyes I want to see.
To feel the warmth you must draw nigh, just
    trust in me, I'd never lie.
Your eyes speak of the pain within; you need my
    love, it isn't sin.
Give me a chance to warm your heart; scoot
    closer now, that's right. Be smart.

"There we go, feel better now. The warmth I
    send upon your brow.
My fire is sweet, will ease your mind, soothe your
    soul just in time.
What's that you say? It's not that hot. You've just
    grown used to that very spot.

Creep a little closer, don't hesitate. You won't
    get burned, come on, don't wait.
The fire crackles, the logs they burn, but you're okay,
    you're smart, you've learned.
To stay away from the fervent heat, just warm
    your hands and toast your feet.
What's that you say? A spark has flown and
    burned your heart, the pain has grown.
It's okay, don't grow shy. I'm here to tell the
    reason why.

"Look around the fire that I've made. There's
    Bill and Susan, your friends; they've stayed.
It's clear that all enjoy the heat. Here come some
    more to take a seat.
That's good. Calm down. Here take my hand, to
    another place. I've got a plan.
Sit here, yes, here upon this spot. It's safer now,
    it's not that hot.
My fire is best, I know it's true. Don't listen to
    what they say to you.
The righteous say you'll burn with me. It's all a
    lie, just wait and see."

About that time the flames burst forth, it's a
    raging fire from another source.
Hell itself has opened wide
    to take your soul to the other side.
The devil laughs. The demons grin, as another
    pays the price for sin.
Licked by the fire you scream in pain, what you
    would give for a gentle rain.
You hear the moans of the suffering crowd, you
    cannot believe that you've allowed
The devil's lies to take you down to the fiery
    inferno below the ground.

There is a lesson here for all to learn, don't play
    with sin, the fire will burn.
You still have time to make it right; reach out to
    Jesus this very night.
He'll pluck you from the scorching flames, mend
    your wounds to never be the same.
He's here tonight to set you free, but it's up to
    you. What will it be?

Sin is like fire. We all have probably heard the parental warning, "Son, if you play with fire, you'll get burned!" It's the same with sin. If you play with sin, you're going to pay the consequences—and they are severe.

Fires often start innocently and become catastrophic within seconds. How many millions of acres of America's timberland have been destroyed by the thoughtless flip of a cigarette out a car window, or by the failure of campers to properly douse their campfire? How many lives and homes have been lost to fires ignited by people celebrating with fireworks? These people usually have no idea that their bottle rockets landed in a field of tall, dry, fire-hungry grass or their neighbor's sun-dried, wood-shingle roof!

It is the same with sin, friend. Sin, like fire, almost always starts innocently, but before long it becomes catastrophic. Sinners never expect to become hardened or do the things they do. Young people never think about the consequences when they pick up that first joint of marijuana or drink their first beer—they would never believe they could become a drug addict or alcoholic. That always happens "to other people." They don't realize they are holding a match from hell in their hands.

They are lighting a brush fire that could create a blazing inferno—and they don't even know it.

The inferno really begins the moment that little match of sin is struck and the first tiny spark appears. Do you know what I'm talking about? How many prostitutes on our streets could trace their path directly to their childhood when they had their first sexual encounter at the tender age of 13? Little did they know that one day they would be sleeping with men for $50 or less a night, making their living by selling their bodies and souls to hundreds of men a month. They start each day feeling like a tramp and are treated like the scum of the earth, but they didn't start that way. Their destructive bondage started with a little fire that often seemed so innocent. (I also realize that many young women who become prostitutes were victimized by their fathers, uncles, cousins, and other abusive men.) No young lady ever enters into a love affair with a young man believing she will end up in a maternity ward or abortion clinic months later. Every fire begins with a tiny spark, friend.

Fires must be fed to continue burning. It is the same with sin. What happens if you stop throwing logs on a fire? It will go out. Firefighters in the timberlands know the only way to put out a major forest fire is to cut a fire break—a large swath of cleared land that separates the burning inferno from fresh forest lands. They use bulldozers, chain saws, axes, and mattocks—anything needed to help remove trees, brush, undergrowth, leaves, and grass from the path of the flames. Their only hope is to deprive the consuming flames of fresh fuel.

This may sound elementary, but all of us need to hear it again and again. If you are still in sin and can't figure out why, I can probably pinpoint the problem: Somehow, in some way, you are still tossing logs on the fire! If you tell me you are losing the battle with a pornography problem, I might ask you, "What do you do when you walk into a neighborhood convenience store? Do you walk over to the magazine racks and scan the top row of magazines? Do you peek behind the cardboard covers to see the provocative covers of "adult" soft-porn magazines? That is a log that only feeds the fire that's burning you. I have a clue for you: Why don't you quit going by the magazine stand? If you don't have any logs around a fire, it will go out.

If you are battling an alcohol problem, are you still driving past your old drinking spot down in the sleazy part of town? Steer clear of the old haunts and old friendships. Drive to your destination using another route. I don't care if it takes longer or uses more gas— what is another buck in gas money if it helps you free yourself from that old garbage from the past? Quit throwing logs on the fire that keeps burning you.

Fire cannot be weighed or measured. Fire (and sin) has no boundaries. It has one nature: to consume. It will consume and destroy everything it can. Its hunger will never be satisfied.

Fire is not selective in its destruction. It will destroy anything that is in its path—the beautiful, the ugly, the bright, the dull, the innocent, the guilty. Satan and sin are the same way. The Bible says, "Be sober, be vigilant; because your adversary the devil, as a roaring lion, walketh about, seeking whom he may devour" (1 Pet. 5:8). I've watched people fall into sin and failure by the thousands in this nation; millions are in a backslidden condition, great preachers have toppled from their thrones, and laymen have fallen into sin. The fire of sin has burned the great and the small, the rich and the poor, the preacher and the prostitute with equal glee. Even the innocent have been targeted for destruction.

Little kids are getting hooked on pornography through the Internet; they are being introduced to masturbation when they are only nine and ten years old. The sins of child molestation and deviant sexual compulsions are raging across this nation, burning and scarring the hearts of countless innocent victims every day. Sin has no boundaries.

Perhaps you have started a little bitty fire in a private field where no one can see you. "It's just a little bitty thing," you say. If I were sitting across from you right now, would you find it hard to look at me because of the conviction you feel? Why? It is because you started something years ago that seemed like a little thing, an innocent flirtation, a childish whim. Now it has exploded out of proportion. Ask yourself how an affair begins? Does it begin in a bed of adultery? No, it starts at the water cooler at the office or at the food court in the mall.

You looked too long and with too much interest at the attractive lady who orders a hamburger there every day. Finally, you winked back and sat down to eat your meal with her. That's how an affair starts. It starts with a tiny spark when a match is struck. When you saw that woman again, you threw another little twig on the delicate flame, and the next time you threw a larger branch of illicit interest on the growing fire. Before you knew it, the growing fires of passion were no longer content with twigs and small branches; they propelled you into the woman's bed and quickly reached out to consume your marriage and your family! Your whole life came apart at the seams while you shook your head in disbelief and lamented, "I didn't know. I didn't recognize the danger in the beginning." I'm warning you now, friend: Don't play with sin's fire.

The second major point of this message is that *many people are suffering from severe burns.* If you are suffering from burns inflicted by sin and past mistakes, then in Jesus' name, I'm going to pull you from the fire. Perhaps you haven't delved deep enough into sin to be burned, but you have experienced some smoke damage. You have been close to the fire, but you are not into it yet. There is an old saying that goes, "Where there's smoke, there's fire." If a person's clothing smells like smoke, then he's been around a fire of some sort.

Parents know what I'm talking about. They know something is up when Johnny comes home one night looking "different." His clothes smell funny and something just doesn't seem to be right. Melissa has suddenly lost that sweet countenance she had before she went to the prom. You smell smoke but you don't see any fire yet. If you ask your daughter, "Honey, have you been smoking marijuana?" and she says, "No, Mom, I haven't," she might be telling the truth. "Honey, have you been drinking?" "No, Mom, I haven't." "Honey, this is awkward, but I only know one way to say it. Have you been sleeping around with any guys?" "No, Mom, trust me; I haven't." Mom, perhaps your daughter hasn't, *but she is getting close!* She smells like smoke, so she has been around a fire somewhere.

Some of you have been playing close to the fire, but you haven't touched the flame yet. I can smell the telltale fragrance of smoke on your clothes. You go to the parties, but you don't get drunk. You hang out with some influential, hardened, sin-bitten people, but your clothes have not yet caught on fire. You can feel the heat, but you are still just a little cautious. I'm warning you: You're going to get burned.

The Book of Jude has mandated me to pull you out of the flames. I smell smoke on your clothes—maybe you are just flirting with the idea of an affair, or toying with a forbidden fantasy. Where there is smoke, there is fire, and the devil is setting you up for an encounter with a blazing bonfire. He wants to move you closer little by little to the edge of hell, then he will drop you in. I've watched it thousands of times.

I'm also determined to pull you from the fire if you have already been singed. You have played with fire and were burned a little bit, though your clothes are not ablaze. You have first-degree burns, the mild kind of burns characterized by heat, pain, and redness of the burned area. You are not blistering, and your tissues have not been charred, but you are experiencing some extreme discomfort. You felt the heat of the fire, but you are still hanging around it. I'm ready to help you right now, friend, but you will have to want my help.

A good number of the people reading this book have already suffered second-degree burns. They have been seared by sin, a condition marked by hardness, dryness, and altered appearance, because of the heat of the sin's flame.

*Now the Spirit speaketh expressly, that in the latter times some shall depart from the faith, giving heed to seducing spirits, and doctrines of devils; speaking lies in hypocrisy; **having their conscience seared** with a hot iron* (1 Timothy 4:1-2).

Some translators say these consciences are as dead as seared flesh, or branded with the devil's signs, branded as the devil's slaves, or even burned to a crisp. If you have been seared, then the area of your wound has lost all sensitivity. You are plagued by pain, blistering, scarring, and the destruction of your skin. What has sin done to you? Every night I watch people come into this revival with second-degree burns all over their body. You can see it on their faces, mirrored in the misery, pain, and destruction they've suffered and still carry in their hearts and minds. They have been out there playing with fire too long. It is grace that brought you to this chapter of this book and to the relief offered in Christ.

If you have been seared by satan, then your affair with fire is becoming more serious now. The devil has snagged you, and he is burning you good. You know exactly what I'm talking about. You are in so much pain and misery that you don't know what to do anymore. You are losing strength and you're saying things like, "What's the use?"

I am also out to snatch you from the fire if you have been scorched and wounded by sin with third-degree burns. You are the one in that burning house. The fires are blazing all over your body, and your skin is smoldering. A third-degree burn goes way past the outer layer of skin, way past the dermis. It penetrates deeply into the muscle layers and other internal tissues. A burn of this magnitude actually dries up the moisture inside the body. Everything becomes crusty. Many people who come to the revival at Brownsville are so dry, so burned by sin that they literally cry out, "God, I'm dying! Help me somehow, God." The clothing of their souls is ablaze with the devil's flames. Their only hope is to be plucked from the flames by a sovereign hand.

It is time for the smoky, singed, scorched, and seared to be snatched from the devil's bonfire! God has decreed that is time for His rain to come down. It is time for the hurting to be transformed and translated from the heat of hell to the showers of Heaven.

The Lord has come to pluck, pull, or snatch the sinner out of the fire. Are you getting burned or singed by the fires of sin? There are only two ways you can be saved from a fire: Either put out the fire or escape from the fire. Since man cannot extinguish the fire of sin in his own strength, he must be pulled or snatched out of the flames.

The Church is like a huge volunteer fire department. What were you taught to do if your clothing catches fire? Nearly every elementary kid can tell you: Stop, Drop, and Roll. If you have come too close to the fires of sin and you feel the heat of the flames, friend, then you need to stop what you are doing, drop everything, and roll down to the altar of repentance. God will set you free, but you have to follow His commands.

I read of a fire that broke out in the mental ward of a hospital in England in 1903. There were 300 men and women in what they called an insane asylum. Fifty perished and 250 were literally pulled out of the fire. The descriptions of the way those mental patients behaved throughout the rescue graphically reminded me of the way insane sinners behave when others try to receive salvation through Christ. The similarities are chilling.

Some of the inmates laughed at the mention of fire. Only fools or the mentally infirm could laugh at a calamity like that. Fools make a mock at sin. Only those who are morally insane would dare to trifle with the fire of sin. Some of those inmates laughed, just as many unbelievers will mock the preacher who tries to save them from a house of sin engulfed in satan's flames. In Acts 17 the Bible says that when Paul preached the gospel of Jesus Christ to the philosophers on Mars' hill, some mocked, others hesitated, and others believed. They were basically saying, "That stuff about Christ rising from the dead is a bunch of malarkey. You must be out of your mind." Others said, "We will hear you again on this, Paul." When the apostle left, the Bible also says that some believed and followed him (see Acts 17:22-34).

Some of the those mental patients in England laughed as the hospital was burning down. Some said they would not leave their bed in the night and go out. They were afraid to leave their safety zone— even if it meant they would lose their lives. Many unsaved people prefer the pleasures of their condemned state to the joys of salvation. The reason I like this story is because these people in the mental ward had people who cared about them. The rescuers risked their lives to save them, even though these patients sometimes fought and cursed them. Sinners are just like that. They are "spiritually" insane. When you try to help them, they may curse you. That's insane; that's crazy.

If you try to help them overcome chronic alcoholism, they will tell you with defiance, "It's my life. I can do what I want with it. Now leave me alone!" It's insane. The parallels between the mental patients during that fire and the unsaved are countless. The rescuers found some of the patients hiding under their beds. How many people are hiding under their fluffy beds of religion hoping that the flames of hell won't burn them? Their "refuge of lies" said, "Peace and safety," but only sudden destruction awaited them (see 1 Thess. 5:3). How many are hiding from the truth all over America? They hope that maybe they will make it to Heaven, but they just can't believe there's a hell. So every day we find these persons huddled under religion telling themselves, "There just can't be a fire." God says there is a fire.

Some of those mental patients believed that the staff and the rescuers had started the fire! Some people today believe that preachers are the creators of hell and that they are just disturbing the peace with their preaching. Since we are the ones who are saying, "Fire, fire," they claim we started it! They shout back, "There is nothing wrong with same-sex marriage. Shut up; there is nothing wrong with my pornography problem. It's my life, I can do what I want." Fire, fire, fire! There is a fire in America's house, friend. Sound the alarm. There's only one way out.

Many of the mental patients fought against the very rescuers who were sacrificing themselves for their deliverance. They bit them and tore their hair out. What a sad proof of insanity. Every pastor can tell you sad tales of people who cursed them, fought them, and did everything they could to drive them away— even though they were working for their eternal good.

Every sane man and woman present went to the rescue of these hospital patients. Time was short; if nothing was done, the doom of the remaining souls was certain. The work was great and urgent. Every other task was set aside. The one thing that mattered was the rescue of those poor souls from the fire's flames. Every sane Christian needs to make it his chief business to pull souls out of the fire of sin. Are you out or are you in? If you have sin in your heart and you want to be free, I have good news for you: Jesus Christ said He came to destroy the works of the devil (see 1 Jn. 3:8b), and He did just that 2,000 years ago for you. But you have to make up your mind that you don't want to live in sin and be burned. You need to set your course to live a clean and holy life.

The fire alarm has sounded: there's fire in the house. It is time to escape the flames of sin. Don't complain about the irritating volume of God's alarm—it is the sound of your salvation. God's Word in the Book of Jude told me to sound the alarm as loudly and as long as I can. God has commanded me to devote my life to pulling burn victims from the flames of sin. I suppose God could have used a "softer, gentler" alarm, but He chose me and told me to preach loudly and urgently. I don't preach a "toned down" or politically correct gospel; I just shout at the top of my lungs, "There's fire in the house! Get out while you can!"

If there is sin in your life, then I *guarantee you* that if you stay where you are, you will be burned! The fire will increase, and the damage to your body and soul will move quickly from first-degree to second-degree burns. However, there is no need for it—the Holy Ghost wants to rain on you, soothe your pain and misery, and dry your tears. There are no other options. Either move away from the flame of sin or plan on feeling unspeakable pain.

Every single night of the Brownsville Revival, we see people come in who are spiritually burned crisp. They come in fried, burned out, and sick and tired of sin, but they walk out as white as snow, as brand spanking new creatures. God's Word declares, "Therefore if any man be in Christ, he is a new creature: old things are passed away; behold, all things are become new" (2 Cor. 5:17). I've watched the miracle happen over and over again.

If you want to be snatched from the flames of sin in your life, then move away from the fire! Move closer to Jesus Christ if you need forgiveness and cleansing. He will heal and restore you. Now I've done everything I can do to sound the alarm. I smell smoke in the House of God and throughout the world. Where there's smoke, there's fire. I've already shared the poem entitled "The Devil's Bonfire." I've explained that the devil wants to take you to hell and burn you raw. He came to destroy and kill you. I have warned you about the dangers of sin, and I have told you about the love of Jesus Christ.

Now it is up to you. If you are tired of being burned by sin, then pray this prayer out loud right where you are:

Dear Jesus, thank You for speaking to my heart. Thank You, Jesus, for not leaving me alone in my burning house. Thank You, Lord, for sounding the alarm and for rescuing me. Thank You for redeeming me. Thank You, Lord, for setting me free from the fires of sin and the endless misery of eternal damnation. Right now, I confess that I have sinned. I have hurt You, and I have hurt others. Please forgive me, Jesus. I repent of my sins. Wash me clean and make me new. I give You my ashes in return for beauty. Be my Savior, my Lord, and my very best friend. From this moment on, I am Yours and You are mine. Thank You, Jesus, for removing the scent of smoke from my spiritual life. I am free in You. In Your precious name I pray. Amen.

Chapter 9

A Time to Be Born and a Time to Die

Your birth was a divine appointment. So was mine. I was born on January 17, 1954, in an army hospital in Ankara, Turkey, around 11:00 p.m. The moment that I passed through my mama's birth canal and stuck my little head out into the world, I became recorded history. Stephen Hill was born. The event was so important that they wrote it on a piece of paper. There is a time to be born.

John Wesley was born June 26, 1703. Abraham Lincoln was born February 12, 1809, in a log cabin. Adolph Hitler was born April 20, 1889, in Austria. Henry Ford was born July 30, 1863, in Dearborn, Michigan. John F. Kennedy was born May 29, 1917, in Brooklyn, Massachusetts. Jesse James was born September 5, 1847. George Burns was born January 20, 1896. Richard Nixon was born January 9, 1913. Jerry Garcia, the former lead guitarist of the Grateful Dead was born August 1, 1942. There is a time to be born. Do you understand that the moment you came into this world, it was recorded in history, and it is recorded in the documents of Heaven. God ordained the very moment you were born.

Look back at the list of notable people I've listed. As you read it, do you realize that *at the moment of their birth* they were not presidents, guitar players, mass murderers, great preachers, or legendary actors—they were each just newborns entering a new world. According to wise King Solomon, there is an appointed time to be born.

> *To every thing there is a season, and a time to every purpose under the heaven: a time to be born, and a time to die; a time to plant, and a time to pluck up that which is planted; a time to kill, and a time to heal; a time to break down, and a time to build up; a time to weep, and a time to laugh; a time to mourn, and a time to dance; a time to cast away stones, and a time to gather stones together; a time to embrace, and a time to refrain from embracing; a time to get, and a time to lose; a time to keep, and a time to cast away; a time to rend, and a time to sew; a time to keep silence, and a time to speak; a time to love, and a time to hate; a time of war, and a time of peace* (Ecclesiastes 3:1-8).

Solomon also said, "He hath made every thing beautiful in His time: also He hath set the world in their heart, so that no man can find out the work that God maketh from the beginning to the end" (Eccles. 3:11). There is a time to be born and a time to die. Nothing takes God by surprise. He knew about you before you were born.

I'll never forget the look on Jeri's face (and she'll never forget the astonishment in my face) when we found out that a child was being formed in her womb for the fourth time. We had two children at the time, which we had adopted in Argentina. In past years we had already lost three children through miscarriage and a dangerous tubal pregnancy. Each time I thought she was going to die. Finally, we accepted the possibility that Jeri would never get pregnant again. Then it happened—Jeri was carrying a baby in her womb, and we wanted to know everything. We wore out the doctor with endless questions about everything concerning our baby's growth: "How's the heart? Can you see all the parts? How about the legs? The arms? Now how about the little head—is everything okay?"

Our little baby was only about the size of a walnut at the time, but we wanted to know everything. The doctor couldn't answer all of our questions in the first few weeks, but God already knew the details. The doctor said our little daughter would be born sometime around May 27, but God knew that little Kelsey Noel would be born at exactly 1:00 p.m. on May 29! There is a time to be born. It was the same with Kelsey's big brother and sister, Ryan and Shelby. God knew exactly when you would be born too. You aren't here by mistake. Nothing takes God by surprise, and His calendar is jammed with appointments.

Today, during the next 24 hours, almost a half a million people will be born into this world. Eleven thousand of those people will be born in the United States of America, and four million people will be born in this country this year alone. There is a time to be born. I don't know about you, but I'm glad that God's ordained time for my birth came in the 1900's instead of the 1500's. I love all the great preachers of old, but many of them only lived to be 40 years old. They died early. Robert Murray McCheyne died at the young age of 30. He walked the earth for three decades and then entered his grave. I mention him all the time in my ministry, but he only lived seven years for Jesus before he was dead and gone. Why? Because of rampant sickness in an age when there was little or no medicines. Most people died early. I'm also glad I wasn't born back in the 1800's. I'm glad I don't have to wash clothes on a washboard at the river. I'm glad I don't have to spend half the day out hunting for game with a shotgun or rifle so my family can eat supper. (Thank God for grocery stores.)

I love to talk to teenagers about Old Testament times. The Scriptures say there is a time to be born and a time to die, but if we lived in that time virtually every teenager and most adults I speak to these days would be dead by now because of rebellion! The Old Testament treatment for rebellion was permanent. It was a 100 percent cure, but the patient rarely survived. The Book of Deuteronomy outlined the treatment:

> *If a man have a stubborn and rebellious son, which will not obey the voice of his father, or the voice of his mother, and that, when they have chastened him, will not hearken unto them: then shall his father and his mother lay hold on him, and bring him out unto the elders of his city, and unto the gate of his place; and they shall say unto the elders of his city, This our son is stubborn and rebellious, he will not obey our voice; he is a glutton, and a drunkard. And all the men of his city shall stone him with stones, that he die: so shalt thou put evil away from among you; and all Israel shall hear, and fear* (Deuteronomy 21:18-21).

Things could be pretty tough for the teenager who eats donuts all day and refuses to mow the yard. I think under this plan most of the people in any congregation would have been "put away" before they reached adulthood. I know my hand would have to go up. How about yours? Would you have been a dead rebel? I thank God I wasn't born back then.

There is a time to be born, but the Bible also says there is a time to die. Everybody is going to die. You are not dead yet. Your time has not come, but your time is coming. You have an appointment that cannot be broken. It is your destiny to die.

The time span between the time you take your first breath to the moment you take your last is very, very short. Did you know that this year 2,500,000 people will drop dead in the United States of America? Most of these people will die without a clue about why and how quickly it will happen. Seven hundred fifty thousand will die of heart disease, and 550,000 will drop dead of cancer. Strokes will claim another 160,000 (that is how Leonard Ravenhill died. One day he was perfect; the next minute he was barely hanging on, then he slipped into eternity with Jesus). Over 200,000 will die in automobile accidents or home accidents. Some will trip down a stairway and break their necks, and others will have a fatal accident on a bicycle. Almost 250,000 people will die like that. Another 250,000 U.S. citizens will die this year from some other type of disease. AIDS will claim 50,000, and suicide will snuff out 35,000 souls. The time span between your first and last breath is short. The Bible says life is but a dream that flies away, a shadow that disappears, a cloud that vanishes, a flower that dies, and as grass that withers.

You were born to fulfill an eternal purpose. You don't know how much time you have left, but whatever you do, make it count. The Bible says this life is like a vapor that vanishes. It is as a mere breath. We don't have the space to track down each of these descriptions in the Bible, but they are all there. Life is short— even in the United States where advanced medical technology has made us believe the lie that we will live forever. It just won't happen. In 1920, just before the Great Depression, the average life expectancy was 54 years. Now the average American lives to the age of 74. So we have advanced 20 years, and I don't believe we will do much better than that on the average. God promised us "seventy plus ten years" (see Ps. 90:10) if we are real healthy. Medical advances can only slightly delay the inevitable— God's Word says there is a time to be born and a time to die. So whether you have smooth skin or wrinkled skin, one day you will die.

I remember holding a missions convention in Canada with former astronaut James Irwin. He was a great Christian. He was born back in 1930, and he watched technology take us from the Model T Ford to the Apollo spacecraft that took him to the moon. Brother Irwin spent 67 hours on the moon, and he even left the lunar landing module to take a walk while he was up there. James Irwin was the epitome of health. He was full of "vim and vigor," and when I looked at him I thought, *I can just picture this guy jumping around on the moon.*

Jim didn't slow down after he left the NASA space program. He devoted a number of years trying to find Noah's ark on Mount Ararat. He took research teams over there several times, and he even scaled the mountain itself in search of clues. This was James Irwin, the astronaut, the perfect picture of health. Everywhere he traveled he took a portable bicycle that he would whip out and bolt together. He pedaled that thing all over the place. It seemed like he was always jogging or riding his bike. Then one day this seemingly invincible guy in perfect health was riding his bicycle when he suddenly fell over and died of a massive heart attack. On August 8, 1991, James Irwin's memorable life was over. For both the great and the small there is a time to be born and a time to die. I am thrilled to tell you that when James Irwin died, he was ready. He was on fire for God. When he fell off that bike, he landed right in the loving arms of Jesus. He's got a better view now than he ever had on the moon or in the Apollo spacecraft.

I mentioned John Wesley earlier in this chapter. That great soul-winner and church planter was born into time like you and me, but he also died, on March 2, 1791. Abraham Lincoln was born like everyone else, but he also died on April 15, 1865, right across the street from the Ford Theater in Washington, D.C., where he had been struck down by an assassin's bullet. Adolf Hitler was born, but he also died. He was born in lovely Austria, but he died by his own hand on April 30, 1945, in a cold bunker in Berlin. Henry Ford was born like you were, but he also died on April 7, 1947. John F. Kennedy was born just like I was, but then there was a fatal shot. President Kennedy died at the hands of a sniper on November 22, 1963, at 12:30 p.m. in a Dallas hospital. John F. Kennedy breathed his last breath surrounded by surgeons, nurses, and his wife; then it was over. The Presidential limousine left the hospital without him.

There is a time to be born and a time to die. Jesse James died on April 3, 1882. George Burns, a man everyone thought would live forever, slipped into eternity on Saturday, March 9, 1996. Jerry Garcia, the lead guitarist for the group, The Grateful Dead, was considered one of the greatest guitarists in the rock music world. His cult of followers included thousands of fans from all over the world. My brother had worked with The Grateful Dead, and he idolized Jerry Garcia. However, Garcia died on

August 9, 1995. He is gone forever. There is a time to be born and a time to die.

God has placed eternity in your heart, a deep inner longing to know Him. You sense this longing from the moment you are born. That is why you can walk into a children's worship service and hear little kids singing, "Yes, Jesus loves me! Yes, Jesus loves me!" That is why little kids will come up and say, "Mommy, I gave my heart to Jesus." "Are you sure, Billy? How old are you now?" "I'm four, and I gave my heart to Jesus." Why? The Lord has put eternity into our hearts.

We all know that we will not live forever. We know the time will come when this old collection of flesh and bones will go back to where it came from. You are dirt, and you will return to dirt. Yet God Almighty has put something inside you. I know what I'm talking about. If you go to a bar tonight in your hometown, you will hear people talking about Jesus. They will be talking about Him over their martinis, their gin and tonics, and their bourbon. Do you want to know why? God has put His eternity into their hearts. Even the hardest individuals have moments when they say to themselves, "There is something out there. There has to be something more to this. There is something more to life than what I have experienced."

Ninety-two percent of all Americans have a Bible in their homes. Now if you went into their homes and told them you wanted their Bible, I believe most of them wouldn't give it up! Why? There is something about that Bible that touches the eternity in their hearts. They know there is something in that book, and that is what keeps it on the mantel by the fireplace. They may be living for the devil and burning the midnight oil trying to make a buck out there. They may be living off the fat of the land, with no regard to God. They may even be agnostic God haters, but they will still have a Bible in their home. Why? Eternity is in their hearts.

The booming psychic channels on television are skyrocketing because people know there is something more out there somewhere. There are 6,000 different cults operating in Japan alone, and I imagine there are at least 10,000 cults in America! Why? Everyone knows or senses there is "something" out there. More than 750,000,000 people believe that Jesus is the Son of God—because He has put eternity in their hearts. That's what draws you to Jesus—you know there has to be more to life and eternity than merely walking around on this planet for 70 years.

"Eat, drink, and be merry for tomorrow we die. Get yourself a little plot of land, put up a little tent shack, drive a Volkswagen, go to work, eat a steak every now and then, scarf down McDonald's hamburgers!" Is that all there is to life? Give me a break! You *know* there is *more*. Why are there more than one billion Muslims in the world? Because they know there is something more out there. Why are there 746,000,000 Hindus on this planet? Because they know there is something more out there. Why are there 332,000,000 Buddhists on the earth? Because they know there is something more out there. Why are there 2,700,000 Baha'is today? Because there is something more out there.

I understand there are also 900,000,000 atheists in the world, although I've never met one. I have met a lot of people who told me they were atheists, but I really want to be there when they stand the test. They entered the world by God's appointment, an event that gave them the privilege of claiming their Maker doesn't exist. But whether they believe it or not, the same Creator has decreed that they will face another appointment soon. What will they say when they are lying on their deathbed with tubes in their nose and throat, IV's in their veins, and surviving on a ventilator machine? What will they do when the doctor says, "Fred, you've been in a serious accident. Your wife and daughter are dead, and your son is on life support two rooms over. You only have a few minutes to live, Fred. Is there anyone you would like to talk to?"

I don't think old Fred is going to call in his business partner and tell him to take care of the business. Why? He has eternity in his heart. Fred will start talking about God, friend. "If You are out there, God...." He will begin to cry out to the One who placed eternity in his heart.

Thousands of folks are going to die today in this nation. Why? Their time is over. There is a time to be born and a time to die. Are you ready to die? John Wesley was born, lived his life for God, and died. He gave his life to the Lord as a little boy after his house burned down. His life was dedicated to God by Susanna Wesley, his mama. There was a time for him to be born and a time to die. But look at what he did in the middle of it! God placed eternity in John Wesley's heart. He knew that life is a shadow. It is just a fleeting moment, so he dedicated his life to the Lord Jesus Christ.

You have the same opportunity. You can breathe, you are alive, you can think, you can walk, you can talk. You can still make decisions. Jesus Christ died for you so He could give you life in abundance. Eternal life is within your grasp this very moment. Do you know that everybody on this planet is going to live forever? It's true. We may die a physical death, but the "real you" will live forever in one of two places: Heaven or hell.

The decision you make on the earth dictates where you will spend eternity. God has appointments. "And as it is appointed unto men once to die, but after this the judgment" (Heb. 9:27). I've watched people get saved a mere six feet away from where I was preaching, only to hear that they had suddenly died one or two weeks later. They were snatched from the flames in the nick of time. They got on fire for God one week and were hit broadside by a tractor trailer rig on the highway the next. They were instantly transported into glory. While they were in the revival services, they heard the preacher preach, they heard the songs of praise being sung, and they felt the pull of eternity in their hearts. They realized that this life is fleeting, and that they needed to do something about their lives. They wanted something better than what they had, so they received Jesus Christ as their personal Savior. They were ready for whatever would come.

What are you going to do now? You may be "close," but it doesn't matter how close you are unless you grasp Him. You have to grasp eternal life. You have to grasp Jesus Christ to be saved. Don't talk to me about religion or church membership. Church membership is a lot like a radio contest I was involved with as a young man. A local radio station was giving away a brand new candy-apple red Honda 450 motorcycle (the largest available at that time), and all you had to do was find the key to the thing in a hidden place somewhere in the city. The station would broadcast 50 clues, and it was up to the listeners to find the key.

I listened to all the clues, and my brother and I thought we knew exactly where that key was located. It had something to do with a golf course, and the golf course was right there. Another clue said it had something to do with a rocket, and there was a model rocket right in the middle of this park. Another clue had something to do with a fallout shelter, and there was a fallout shelter close by. One clue mentioned a highway—yup. Another one talked about a drive-in theater—yup. We had it all figured out. We knew we were close, but we hadn't touched the key yet. I remember sitting on the corner of a cement slab right next to the fallout shelter, and asking my brother, "Where is that key?" We looked everywhere for that thing. Finally I got so frustrated that I went home. A few minutes after I left the park, a young man reached right underneath the corner of the concrete slab where I had been sitting and pulled out the key.

Are you like that? Are you sitting there with this book in your hand and the power of God flooding the room, saying, "God, when are You going to touch my life? When are You going to change me? When are You going to do something for me? Aw, what's the use?" Don't get up and walk away today. I can guarantee that the Lord is saying to you, "The key is right there—it's right in front of you. Reach out and grab it."

Many people who read these words will face eternity in only a matter of months after they open this book. There is a time to be born and a time to die. Mark my words. Some who read this page will think, **Que sera sera**—*what will be will be*. But they won't face death like that. They will face death with trembling. God has placed His love, His peace, His joy, and His tender mercy right in front of you. All you have to do is reach out to Jesus Christ, the Lamb of God who takes away the sin of the world. He is the One who died for you 2,000 years ago. He knows everything about what you are going through.

Jesus faced death and died so that when you face death, you will welcome it with open arms. I told my wife that I am ready to die at any time. She knows it. I would love to go be with Jesus right now. I welcome death. Yes, I am a responsible man. I love my family and my kids, but I love Jesus more than anything on the face of this earth. If my time to die comes tonight or tomorrow, I am ready. There is a time to be born and a time to die. Are you ready?

Examine yourself and ask: "Am I ready to die? If my life was taken from me, where would I spend eternity?" John Wesley went to be with the Lord when he died, but there have been countless others who did not. I am not their judge, but according to the fruits of their lives and the confessions of their mouths, Heaven was not the destination of Adolf Hitler, Jesse James, or many of the rock idols who have recently died. I'm not a judge of any man, but I'm not a fool. I'm not one of those preachers who will lie at your son's funeral. If your son was living in sin, then I won't stand up at the funeral and say he was a good boy. I'll turn to you and say, "I can't preach your son's funeral unless you let me tell the truth and allow me to present an altar call at that funeral. I need to tell the truth about what he was doing because all his friends are going to be there. If I lie about Bill or Bobby or Johnny, they will know I'm lying because they knew him." There is a time to be born and a time to die. Abe Lincoln was born in a log cabin and buried in a President's tomb. They come and they go, don't they? Your turn is coming.

You need forgiveness if your heart is not right with God. Now is your chance. Today is the day of salvation. Come to Jesus and get right with God. This is your time. Yesterday is gone, and tomorrow may never come. Now is all that you have for certain. Most important of all, the Spirit of the Lord has been dealing with you.

Are you doing things that grieve the Lord? If you should die after you lay down this book and walk away, where will you land on the other side of eternity? If you have a "religious" background, then you are like I was the day I was sitting on that concrete slab with the key hidden right underneath me. It doesn't matter what position your father or mother held in what church or religious organization—it won't help you the day you die. It doesn't matter that you had perfect attendance in Sunday school and summer church school—if you aren't right with God, you won't be able to welcome death when your time comes. Your daddy can be a preacher, but you will still burn if you can't answer the question, "Do you know the Lord?" If you were on a jet airliner, about to crash, would you have to repent—or would you worship? Would you scream out, "Oh God, forgive me...wash my sins away!" Or would you lift your hands and say, "Jesus, we're all about to die. Into Thine hands I commit my spirit." Are you ready to die? I'm asking you straight because we will all stand before God on Judgment Day. When you look over at me, you will remember the message I wrote on these pages. You will remember that I warned you about this day.

You need to make a public confession of your faith and dependence on Jesus, because if you can't do it publicly, then you are ashamed of the Lord. And if you are ashamed of the Lord today, He will be ashamed of you on Judgment Day (see Mt. 10:32-33). That's Bible, and it is hard fact.

If you are serious about getting right with God, and about devoting the rest of your life—from this moment until your appointed time of death—to the work of God's Kingdom, then I want you to pray this prayer out loud, right where you are:

Dear Jesus, thank You for being so determined to reach me before my appointed days on this earth are over. I acknowledge that I have sinned against You. I have hurt You, and I've hurt others too. Please forgive me. I am sorry for what I've done, and I repent of my sins. Please wash me clean with Your Blood. I dedicate the rest of my days to You—show me what You want me to do and where You want me to go. Thank You for the abundant life in Your presence. From this appointed day on, I am Yours and You are mine. In Your wonderful name I pray, Lord Jesus. Amen.

Chapter 10

The God Seekers

I have a missionary friend who is working in a Bible school in Belarus where we planted a church together. His family is very wealthy, and much of the wealth was earned through the family optical business. This isn't a little "while you wait" lens grinding operation in a shopping mall; it is a major corporation serving the optical industry from coast to coast. When I visited the massive corporate offices, I saw the still-vacant office where my friend once worked. The memories of my friend's commitment to Christ flooded my mind all over again.

One day my friend went to his father and said, "Dad, I love this business, and I love you and Mama. I'm not ashamed to be called your son, and I'm not ashamed of the riches you have earned. God has blessed this business, but Dad, I'm going after Jesus. He is calling me to the mission field, and I don't want this anymore—all I want is God." His dad came up to me shaking his head. "Steve, I don't understand it. My son is climbing in this business. One day he and his brothers will take over the business and he'll have everything. He's been trained for this, and he is really good. He has a great future and everything he could want. Now he doesn't want it—he says he wants to follow God."

I turned to this father, smiled, and said, "Yeah, and aren't you proud of him? Let me tell you something about your sons. You will go off to some optical convention in Dallas or New York. All of your optical friends will be there. You will be sitting at these banquets with all those men and you will all talk about your families. When they ask, 'Well, what about your family?' you'll name your two sons who are working at your side in the optical business and explain with pride how they followed in your footsteps and are continuing a proud family tradition. But then your eyes will just light up when you talk about your third son. 'And then I have a third son who left the business to become a missionary. He is preaching the gospel of Jesus Christ around the world. You know, that boy loves Jesus with all of his heart. He's a God seeker if I've ever seen one.' " This father deeply loved each of his sons—but there is a special honor that follows the God seeker that cannot be matched.

*If My people, which are called by My name, shall humble themselves, and pray, and **seek My face**, and turn from their wicked ways; then will I hear from heaven, and will forgive their sin, and will heal their land* (2 Chronicles 7:14).

The Book of First Chronicles also says, "Seek the Lord and His strength, seek His face continually" (1 Chron. 16:11). Something is happening in America right now. People are going after God, and millions more are going to be saved in the months and years ahead. If you refuse to follow God and choose instead to cling to the past, then you will look back in regret, just like the critics who dismissed Azusa, who ridiculed and mocked the Wesley revivals, and who lambasted Jonathan Edwards. You will be one of those persons who look back and say, "I wish— oh how I wish I had gotten involved in that. That was so much God, and I was so blind."

One of the by-products of this revival is the urge to re-examine and question what we believe. We're not doubting God, but we're asking all the right questions. When we are challenged by the Word during a revival meeting, we begin to analyze ourselves. My friend, that is the healthiest thing you can do. It is good to hear someone say, "That's what we believe, but Lord, that's not what we're preaching or living!" People are praying, "Lord Jesus, I'm so sick of all this church stuff. Who am I? Where do I fit in the scheme of things? Does the devil even know my name? Am I known in hell? Am I a threat to the kingdom of darkness, or is the enemy saying, 'Jesus, I know, and Paul, I know, but who are you?' Does he look at me and laugh?"

On the other side of the fence, there are people who study this revival hoping to find *backsliders*! Why? They want to put them on national news and in religious magazines so they can debunk the work of God in this revival. What if that was your job? What if you made a living by "hunting down people who didn't make it." Dear God, that's the same as being a bounty hunter for the devil! They would have booked Judas on the first available religious talk show, and they would have had a heyday with the folks who walked away after Jesus told them to eat His flesh and drink His Blood in John 6:53-66. *His revival would have definitely made the black list* of questionable revivals. These folks aren't interested in helping these fallen souls find repentance and forgiveness—no, they want to plaster their names and their sins on the nation's airwaves and magazines and say, "See there! Haven't we warned you all along?! Look at her, *she didn't make it*. It can't be God." Friend, if that's you, look closely at the Scriptures that say, "Touch not Mine anointed" (1 Chron. 16:22). Keep your hands off.

It's our time to come to God. We need to stop waiting for God to do something for us—He has already come down to us. He's already sought man. The Bible says, "For God so loved the world, that He gave His only begotten Son" (Jn. 3:16a). God has already come down to man. He did it 2,000 years ago. You're wasting time, friend. He has given you legs to walk, hands to move, a mouth to speak, and ears to hear. It's time for you to move. God has already done His part through Jesus Christ.

Someone said a long time ago, "You can lead a horse to water, but you can't make him drink." Yes, you can, friend: *You can salt his oats.* God has His salt shaker out. People are coming to this revival with terrible attitudes and ever stronger thirsts. At first, many of them hunker down in their pews and just sit there, like stubborn old mules in the middle of the road. They say, "I ain't going to get nothin' from God." Before long, they start licking their lips and swallowing harder. They're thirsty. When the altar call is given, they come running by the hundreds. God salted their oats. Time after time people have testified that they had come to the services to mock us, but it didn't take 30 minutes for the Holy Ghost to get hold of them and bring them to the altar at a run.

A man's desperation for the presence of God will melt all preoccupation with self, notoriety, public image, and social status. Your hunger and thirst, if it is genuine, will drive you to eat and to drink of Him regardless of the opinion of others. You'll be willing to be a fool in the sight of your peers in order to be embraced in the arms of the Lord. This is the first characteristic of a true God seeker.

Number 1:   The God seeker is willing to go after Jesus regardless of the cost.

I have to applaud God seekers who dare to take a stand for Jesus. In 1996, a drama unfolded in the state of Alabama when a small group mounted a fast-paced campaign to remove the Ten Commandments from the wall of the state supreme court building. Alabama Governor Fob James tried everything he could to stop the action. He knew the vast majority of his constituents would be up in arms if a small group of people was able to force their ungodly will on the majority. The Governor's family is among those who have been in favor of this revival and the workings of God throughout the region. Governor James said, "Now, wait just a cotton-pickin' minute! We're not taking down those Ten Commandments." Then he told them, "We're not only not going to take them down, but if the federal government tries to take them down, I'll call in the Alabama National Guard!"

The word quickly got out to other state governors who love God, and Governor James soon received a call from South Carolina. It was the governor of that state. He told Governor James, "Listen Fob, if you need my National Guard, I'll send them too!" Why would he say that, friend? The bottom line is that these leaders are God seekers. They are people who want God. They want Him to move on this nation, and they are willing to go after Jesus—regardless of the cost. It doesn't matter if some liberal governor on the other side of the nation is belly-aching and griping. They don't care if they are blackballed by half the nation—they want God. They want the principles of this country to be laid down on a firm foundation, as they were with our forefathers.

These men are willing to pay the cost to see it happen. We stand with them in the cause of Christ.

Can you say with Peter, "Behold, we have forsaken all and followed Thee..." (Mt. 19:27b)? Peter left his fishing boat (his occupation), and his home. He dared to launch out into the deep with Jesus. Notice what Jesus told Peter and the other disciples: "And every one that hath forsaken houses, or brethren, or sisters, or father, or mother, or wife, or children, or lands, for My name's sake, shall receive an hundredfold, and shall inherit everlasting life" (Mt. 19:29).

Number 2: The God seeker will go after Jesus regardless of how painful his or her present circumstances are.

You may have hit "rock bottom" yesterday or this week. What are you going through, friend? How painful is your situation? Are you going through a divorce or a church split? I'm telling you, *seek God*. Are you battling incredible physical pain? Are you going through the agony of cancer surgery? Perhaps you've already lost your hair through chemotherapy, and right now you are looking ahead at days and days of agony to come. If you are in literal pain, friend, this is the time to look up to Jesus. Remember the thief on the cross who received Christ? Don't forget...he was also being crucified. He was experiencing horrific pain. But he became a God seeker in the midst of his agony. The God seeker will seek the face of Jesus regardless of how painful the present circumstances are.

Number 3: The God seeker is driven by a personal hunger that far excels every other desire in life.

Zacchaeus the rich, chief tax collector appears in Luke 19 in the New Testament. This man had lots of money, very little respect among his countrymen (tax collectors were viewed as traitors who worked to collect taxes for the Roman invaders for personal gain), and was of very short stature. When he wanted to see Jesus, he couldn't get through the thick crowd, and he couldn't see over the taller people. His solution was to shimmy up a sycamore tree right over the road. When Jesus reached the spot under the tree, He looked up and said, "Zacchaeus, make haste and come down; for today I must abide at thy house" (Lk. 19:5b). That was a New Testament altar call, by the way. Put this picture in context. Replace Zacchaeus with any one of the 40 richest men in the nation—put them up in a tree waiting to see Jesus, and you will begin to understand that there was a personal hunger in Zacchaeus that far excelled every other desire in his life. He had been transformed from a money seeker to a God seeker.

One time I was offered a position in a large church along with a hefty salary. At that time I was making $20 a week. That was $40 every two weeks, $60 every three weeks, and $80 every month. No matter how I added it up, I lived broke. Jeri and I mowed yards and raked leaves to pay for our wedding, and later, just to buy the bare essentials. We used to look forward to going out to Burger King because that was our big splurge once a week—to get a hamburger. That was all the money we had. Then I received a phone call from a man who said, "Is this Steve Hill?" "Yes, sir, it is." "I need an associate pastor." "You do? Where are you from?" He told me the name of the church and said, "I just want you to know that we're in the richest neighborhood in town. And this is what we'll start you out at—$35,000 a year. We'll also give you a new car and a home. Just come work with us as the associate pastor." Now for an associate pastor, this is not a bad salary, especially when you're only making $20 a week.

Friend, I didn't even have to think about it. I listened to everything the man had to say, but I knew it was not God. I told him, "Sir, I appreciate it so much. It's an honor to be asked to come on your staff because I am familiar with your church. I know it's a great church, but really, what I'm doing right now is God's will for me." Then I hung up the phone and thought privately to myself, *You fool.* That doubt didn't last long. I had made up my mind to be a God seeker, friend. I wanted God and God alone. It doesn't matter what anyone offers you, friend: *What is God telling you to do?*

Number 4:   The God seeker is not only willing to go after Jesus, but will obey His words when he or she finds Him.

When you come to Jesus, He will continue to talk to you about your life and your choices because He cares about every detail of your life. If you were to get saved today after reading this book, then Jesus would still be talking to you tomorrow, next week, and even ten days later, about some of the harmful things you will have to give up. The goal of your life in Christ is to become like Him. That means *change* will come, and obedience must become part of your life.

According to John's Gospel, Jesus spit on the ground and made a clay paste to anoint a blind man's eyes (I can almost hear the critics scribbling notes for their next position paper). When He had anointed the man's eyes, Jesus said, "Go, wash in the pool of Siloam, (which is by interpretation, Sent.) He went his way therefore, and washed, and came seeing" (Jn. 9:7). Jesus gave this man a command, friend. He had already come to Jesus, but Jesus required him to do something in order to see the transformation completed. A God seeker is willing to obey the words of the Lord.

Number 5: The God seeker maintains an open heart, always ready to embrace new revelation from the Lord.

I remember watching one man who continually smirked and made ugly faces at someone who was dancing in the Spirit during the revival worship service. It was pitiful. We captured the whole thing on videotape. I just wish this man could have seen what he was doing—I think he would have been embarrassed at the looks he was giving his sister in Christ. The problem was that he didn't like what God was doing in that person. He resented the freedom that sister had in the Spirit, and he refused to accept the fact that God delights in our uninhibited worship and praise to His name. The Bible describes two incidents, back to back, of people who responded to new revelations.

And a certain Jew named Apollos, born at Alexandria, an eloquent man, and mighty in the scriptures, came to Ephesus. This man was instructed in the way of the Lord; and being fervent in the spirit, he spake and taught diligently the things of the Lord, knowing only the baptism of John. And he began to speak boldly in the synagogue: whom when Aquila and Priscilla had heard, they took him unto them, and expounded unto him the way of God more perfectly. And when he was disposed to pass into Achaia, the brethren wrote, exhorting the disciples to receive him: who, when he was come, helped them much which had believed through grace: for he mightily convinced the Jews, and that publicly, showing by the scriptures that Jesus was Christ. And it came to pass, that, while Apollos was at Corinth, Paul

having passed through the upper coasts came to Ephe-
sus: and finding certain disciples, he said unto them,
Have ye received the Holy Ghost since ye believed? And
they said unto him, We have not so much as heard
whether there be any Holy Ghost. And he said unto
them, Unto what then were ye baptized? And they said,
Unto John's baptism. Then said Paul, John verily bap-
tized with the baptism of repentance, saying unto the
people, that they should believe on Him which should
come after him, that is, on Christ Jesus. When they
heard this, they were baptized in the name of the Lord
Jesus. And when Paul had laid his hands upon them,
the Holy Ghost came on them; and they spake with
tongues, and prophesied (Acts 18:24–19:6).

Apollos had something going. He was smart and people were listening to him. Thank God this God seeker
was open to new revelation. Apollos had a following. He
was learned, and he was eloquent. Sometimes that is a
prescription for pride and arrogance, but not in Apollos.

And he began to speak boldly in the synagogue: whom
when Aquila and Priscilla had heard, they took him
*unto them, and **expounded unto him the way of God***
***more perfectly**. And when he was disposed to pass into*
Achaia, the brethren wrote, exhorting the disciples to re-
ceive him: who, when he was come, helped them much
which had believed through grace: for he mightily con-
vinced the Jews, and that publicly, showing by the scrip-
tures that Jesus was Christ (Acts 18:26-28).

Apollos did not blow up and say, "Who do you think
you are teaching me something new? I was personally
baptized in the baptism of John. I know about John and
about repentance. That's what I teach— don't give me
any new-fangled revelation." No, Apollos was *teachable*.

So were the Christians at Ephesus. They gladly heard and embraced Paul's teachings on the Holy Ghost. How about you? Do you want to stomp out and write "Ichabod" over the door if you see somebody's hand shake or if somebody worships God a little different from the way your grandpa did? Are you tempted to whisper, "Dear God, it's the devil!" the moment you see something new? Beware. You might hear Jesus tell you, "Ye do err, not knowing the scriptures, nor the power of God" (Mt. 22:29b).

Recently we had a pastor come to the revival for one night. He couldn't stand the revival. He stomped out and went home muttering, "I don't like that." If you feel that way when you encounter something that is new to you, I have to ask you, *Where does that spirit come from? Would God make you so closed and rigid in your heart and spirit that you can't even open up enough to allow Him to do something fresh and new in you?* We don't serve a God in a box, so why have you climbed into one? Even worse, why do you insist that God and His entire Kingdom climb into that thing with you? If you say you are a God seeker yet you insist on clinging to a man-made list of stringent regulations, then may the Lord set you free. It is time to shed that "Pharisee anointing" that tried to crucify Christ Himself. Like Apollos and the disciples at Ephesus, you need to maintain an open heart, and always be ready to embrace new revelation from the Lord.

Number 6: The God seeker is willing to pay the price when persecution comes.

The blind man who was healed by Jesus in John 9:7 passed the first hurdle when he obeyed the command of Jesus and washed his eyes in the pool of Siloam. He faced another hurdle when he was actually persecuted for being healed on a religious holy day! His religious leaders weren't interested in learning about his obvious miracle and glorifying God for it—no, they wanted to find the villain who dared to defy their authority by breaking their precious religious rules. They demanded to know, "Who did that?!" This man stood his ground and told them, "Listen, folks. I don't understand all this. All I know is I once was blind, but now I see." Then he went on to point out the blindness of the religious critics and hypocrites, and they threw him out! (See John 9:17-34.) Right after that, Jesus found him. Friend, anytime somebody throws you out, Jesus will always find you.

If you have sin in your life, you won't have to worry about persecution. You will fit right in. But the Bible plainly warns us, "Yea, and all that will live godly in Christ Jesus shall suffer persecution" (2 Tim. 3:12). Leonard Ravenhill used to say to me, "Steve, people are always upset at those who are one step higher." If you are a pastor and revival comes to your church, remember these words: You will read about yourself in the morning paper. Just count on someone blasting you in the editorial comment section. It comes with the territory of a God seeker.

Too many preachers are so spineless and weak that as soon as a little persecution comes, they belly up and float off like a dead fish. They tell their deacon board, "Listen, we're not going to have revival. Let's just go ahead and continue with things the way they were. All this commotion—this is not good for the church." Friend, revival is the best thing that ever happened to the Church.

The Lord told Pastor John Kilpatrick, "You may lose hundreds, but you'll gain thousands." Today, Brownsville Assembly of God is one healthy church. Eighty percent of Brownsville's members tithe. That is a sure sign they are following Jesus. They're God seekers. When this revival first broke out, there were about 50 or 60 people who promptly left. They never wanted revival, and when it came, they left. Do you know what I appreciate so much about Pastor Kilpatrick? He wrote all of those people a personal letter and just loved them, but he never backed up. He didn't scurry over to them with his tail between his leg and beg them, "Oh, come on back, okay? We'll tone things down a little bit. *Please be part of the church.* Why don't you just come on Sunday mornings, and we'll tone down then." No, friend. He said, "Listen. We're going after God. That's just the way it is." You need to make that decision too, because a great awakening is coming to America.

When a leader dares to take a stand and seek God, the people out there who really want revival say, "Yes! Yes! A man of God. There is a real man of God who has made up his mind and knows what he wants. He is a God seeker." Dear God, we need more of them in this country.

I've been praying with all my heart, "God, would You raise up someone in America, a church in America, that would dwarf everything that we've ever seen at Brownsville? Would You do that, Jesus? Maybe in Kansas, maybe in Oklahoma, maybe in Washington. But raise up a church where the power comes down and suddenly the lame are walking and the deaf are hearing! Do it, Lord!"

I love this revival, friend. We're seeing great miracles, but I want to see more. Maybe your church is the one. Maybe you are the one! Maybe you are faithfully pastoring 35 or 80 people, but God is trying to show you an area where you are not as diligent as you should be. Is He trying to get you to obey in the little things so you can follow Him in full-blown revival? He may want to anoint you for healings, or to literally raise the dead for His glory! I'm sure that would cause your church to grow from its current little building into the local civic center. It doesn't take much, friend, trust me. News travels fast. If God is holding back in your life, your church, your ministry, or your community, ask yourself, "Why?" Make sure you remain open to everything God is saying and revealing today.

God wants to see an entire Kingdom of God seekers spanning the globe. God's glory is pleased to descend on true God seekers, but He will not share His anointing and blessings with sin or rebellion. If you are prepared to *give all* to Him without reservation or preconceived limitations, then He is ready to visit your life with His glory and power. Are you ready to change forever? If you are determined to seek God without limit, then pray this prayer with me as a lifelong commitment to your Maker:

Dear Jesus, I don't want to wind up my life as a stale, dry, and critical shell of "what could have been." I want to enter eternity with my life on fire, with my spirit fresh, and with a heart that is ready to receive anything and everything from You! You alone are my chief joy. My meat and drink are to do Your will above everything else. I repent of my sins and every disobedience of the past. I want You to be more than my Savior, dear Jesus. I ask You to be my sovereign Lord, the Ruler of my life. From this moment on, I dedicate my life to being a God seeker. I will rise in the morning with the name of Jesus on my lips, and I will have God on my heart every moment of each day. I live to worship, serve, and obey Your every command. My every prayer says, "More of You, Lord, I want more of You." Thank You for loving me so much, Lord Jesus. I am totally Yours just as You are mine. In Jesus' name I pray. Amen.

Destiny Image
Revival Books
by Dr. Michael Brown

THE END OF THE AMERICAN GOSPEL ENTERPRISE
In this important and confrontational book, Dr. Michael Brown identifies the sore spots of American Christianity and points out the prerequisites for revival.
Paperback Book, 112p. ISBN 1-56043-002-8 Retail $7.99

FROM HOLY LAUGHTER TO HOLY FIRE
America is on the edge of a national awakening—God is responding to the cries of His people! This stirring book passionately calls us to remove the road-blocks to revival. If you're looking for the "real thing" in God, this book is must reading!
Paperback Book, 294p. ISBN 1-56043-181-4 Retail $9.99

HOW SAVED ARE WE?
This volume clearly challenges us to question our born-again experience if we feel no call to personal sacrifice, separation from the world, and the hatred of sin. It will create in you the desire to live a life truly dedicated to God.
Paperback Book, 144p. ISBN 1-56043-055-9 Retail $7.99

IT'S TIME TO ROCK THE BOAT
Here is a book whose time has come. It is a radical, noncompromising, no-excuse call to genuine Christian activism: intercessory prayer and the action that one must take as a result of that prayer.
Paperback Book, 210p. ISBN 1-56043-106-7 Retail $8.99

WHATEVER HAPPENED TO THE POWER OF GOD
Why are the seriously ill seldom healed? Why do people fall in the Spirit yet remain unchanged? Why can believers speak in tongues and wage spiritual warfare without impacting society? This book confronts you with its life-changing answers.
Paperback Book, 210p. ISBN 1-56043-042-7 Retail $8.99

Available at your local Christian bookstore.

Internet: http://www.reapernet.com

Prices subject to change without notice.

Destiny Image
Revival Books

WHEN THE HEAVENS ARE BRASS

by John Kilpatrick.

Pastor John Kilpatrick wanted something more. He began to pray, but it seemed like the heavens were brass. The lessons he learned over the years helped birth a mighty revival in Brownsville Assembly of God that is sweeping through this nation and the world. The dynamic truths in this book could birth life-changing revival in your own life and ministry!

Paperback Book, 168p. ISBN 1-56043-190-3 (6" X 9") Retail $9.99

WHITE CANE RELIGION
And Other Messages From the Brownsville Revival

by Stephen Hill.

In less than two years, Evangelist Stephen Hill has won nearly 100,000 to Christ while preaching repentance, forgiveness, and the power of the blood in what has been called "The Brownsville Revival" in Pensacola, Florida. Experience the anointing of the best of this evangelist's life-changing revival messages in this dynamic book!

Paperback Book, 182p. ISBN 1-56043-186-5 Retail $8.99

THE POWER OF BROKENNESS

by Don Nori.

Accepting Brokenness is a must for becoming a true vessel of the Lord, and is a stepping-stone to revival in our hearts, our homes, and our churches. Brokenness alone brings us to the wonderful revelation of how deep and great our Lord's mercy really is. Join this companion who leads us through the darkest of nights. Discover the *Power of Brokenness*.

Paperback Book, 168p. ISBN 1-56043-178-4 Retail $8.99

Available at your local Christian bookstore.

Internet: http://www.reapernet.com

Prices subject to change without notice.